"Here's to Jessica!" Mari[a] ___ of soda, and all the cheerlead ___

Just as they were about ___ gether, Jessica's attention was ___ blond girl walking into the Dairi Burger.

"Who's that?" Jessica asked, annoyed that this stranger had interrupted Maria's toast honoring her.

"I don't know, but the guys look like their tongues are about to fall out of their mouths," Lila Fowler teased."

"I don't see what all the fuss is about." Jessica scrutinized the girl who was stealing her thunder. "She looks pretty plain, if you ask me."

"If that's plain, then in my next life I want to be plain," Jean West said, taking a bite of her sundae.

"A diet Coke with lemon, please," Jessica heard the girl say, flipping her hair.

Everyone in the restaurant seemed to hold their breath as she left the restaurant with her order.

Jessica, more annoyed than ever, watched as the girl got into a brand-new white convertible Mazda Miata with "Cheerleader" plates and revved the engine before she pulled out.

I hope I never lay eyes on that girl again, Jessica thought as she pushed away her hot-fudge sundae.

JESSICA QUITS
THE SQUAD

Written by
Kate William

Created by
FRANCINE PASCAL

BANTAM BOOKS
NEW YORK • TORONTO • LONDON • SYDNEY • AUCKLAND

RL 6, age 12 and up

JESSICA QUITS THE SQUAD
A Bantam Book / January 1995

Sweet Valley High® is a registered trademark of Francine Pascal
Conceived by Francine Pascal
Produced by Daniel Weiss Associates, Inc.
33 West 17th Street
New York, NY 10011
Cover art by Bruce Emmett

ISBN: 0-553-56630-X

Published simultaneously in the United States and Canada

Bantam Books are published by Bantam Books, a division of Bantam
Doubleday Dell Publishing Group, Inc. Its trademark, consisting of the
words "Bantam Books" and the portrayal of a rooster, is Registered in
U.S. Patent and Trademark Office and in other countries. Marca
Registrada. Bantam Books, 1540 Broadway, New York, New York 10036.

PRINTED IN THE UNITED STATES OF AMERICA

OPM   0 9 8 7 6 5 4 3 2 1

To Steven Lev Groopman

Chapter 1

"Great job today, girls!" Ken Matthews said as he walked past the booth of cheerleaders at the Dairi Burger on Friday afternoon. "You guys were hot! We couldn't have won that game without you."

"Thanks," Jessica Wakefield said, gladly accepting the compliment for the whole table. Ken was the quarterback for the Gladiators, the Sweet Valley High football team, and he had thrown the pass that clinched the game. With his blond hair and winning smile, he was also one of the cutest guys in the school.

Jessica felt personally responsible for the cheering squad's brilliant performance at the Big Mesa game that afternoon. Even though she shared the title of cocaptain with Robin Wilson, she considered herself the true team leader. After all, she put more time and energy into the squad than Robin did.

Robin was great at the organizational stuff, like paperwork and scheduling practices, but Jessica was the real brains behind the squad. She wrote most of the cheers and choreographed the moves. Still, they were a good team, mainly because there wasn't any rivalry between them. Robin wasn't at all competitive with Jessica. On the contrary, she was just happy to be cocaptain. After all, not so long ago Robin hadn't even been a cheerleader. Jessica remembered the old, chubby Robin Wilson, how she had followed Jessica around like a little puppy dog, wanting to be just like her. But now, after recovering from a scary bout with anorexia, during which she had got much too thin, she had reached a healthy weight and was completely her own person. As far as Jessica was concerned, she was the perfect cocaptain. She helped out just enough and never stole the limelight.

Like today, for instance, Jessica was getting the attention and admiration she felt she deserved. The Dairi Burger was teeming with excitement after the big game. The entire football team was there and dozens of their fans, and everybody was congratulating Jessica on her squad's performance. Nothing made Jessica happier than being in the spotlight—a position she found herself in more often than not. After all, with her beautiful long blond hair, sparkling blue-green eyes, and dynamic personality, Jessica was one of the most popular girls at Sweet Valley High.

But even Jessica had to admit that there was someone else who was equally popular at Sweet Valley High—her identical twin sister, Elizabeth. But she was popular in a different way.

Elizabeth, a serious student, was the editor of the school newspaper, *The Oracle*. She liked to have a good time as much as Jessica did, but Jessica knew Elizabeth thought she and her friends were a little silly—that they were more interested in gossip and parties than in their schoolwork. Which was, of course, true, but who could blame them? Still, despite their differences, Jessica and Elizabeth were as close as two sisters could be.

"I was really proud of all of you today," Jessica said to the cheerleaders as she flipped her hair, aware that she was being watched by a lot of the guys. She felt prettier than ever and couldn't help noticing that one person in particular had his eyes on her: Ken Matthews. Every time she looked up and caught him looking at her, he blushed and looked away.

"I know we've all been working hard in practices, and today our hard work paid off," Jessica said, relishing her role as cocaptain.

"Those new cheers you taught us were great," Annie Whitman said enthusiastically.

"I read about them in *Cheerleading* magazine," Jessica said with pride. "At first I thought they might be too complicated, but you guys didn't have any problem with them."

"That's because you're such a great teacher," Robin said, smiling.

"Here's to Jessica!" Maria Santelli raised her glass of soda, and all the cheerleaders did the same.

Just as they were about to click their glasses together, Jessica's attention was diverted by a stunning blond girl walking into the Dairi Burger. She apparently wasn't the only one to notice her, as a hush had fallen over the entire room.

"Who's that?" Jessica asked, annoyed that this stranger had interrupted Maria's toast honoring her.

"I don't know, but the guys look like their tongues are about to fall out of their mouths," Lila Fowler teased. "They're practically salivating over her."

Lila, who was Jessica's best friend and at times her biggest rival, had a knack for saying the exact thing that would make Jessica's blood boil. This was one of those times. *Why can't she just keep her mouth shut?* Jessica wondered.

"She's certainly creating a big stir," Helen Bradley said as everyone watched the girl make her way over to the take-out counter. "You'd think the entire football team had been hit over the head with a hammer."

"I don't see what all the fuss is about." Jessica scrutinized the girl who was stealing her thunder. "She looks pretty plain, if you ask me."

"If that's plain, then in my next life I want to be plain," Jean West said, taking a bite of her sundae. "Check out that body. You probably don't catch her eating sundaes."

"Hey, Winston, put your eyes back in their sockets," Maria said to her boyfriend, Winston Egbert, the class clown, who was sitting on a stool next to the girls' booth.

"Oh, sorry," Winston said with an impish grin. "I was just trying to read what was on her T-shirt."

"Yeah, right," Maria said, shaking her head. "You know, a gorgeous girl walks into the room, and relatively intelligent males are reduced to cavemen in one second."

"Rick Hunter looks like he's about to fall off his stool," Amy Sutton said.

Jessica hardly heard her, though.

"A diet Coke with lemon, please," she heard the girl say, flipping her hair. Then the newcomer gave a dazzling smile to the kid behind the counter. "And I'd like that with a straw."

"Oh, please," Jessica said to her friends, rolling

her eyes. "A diet Coke with lemon, please," she mimicked, hair flip and all. "And I'd like that with a straw. Gimme a break."

"That's probably how she stays so thin," Jean said as she watched the girl walk toward the door sipping her soda.

Everyone in the restaurant seemed to hold their breath as they watched her walk out the door.

"Whoa, mama!" Bruce Patman yelped as the door swung shut behind her.

"Major babe!" Rick Hunter exclaimed.

Jessica, more annoyed than ever, watched as the girl got into a brand-new white convertible Mazda Miata with "Cheerleader" plates and revved the engine before she pulled out.

I hope I never lay eyes on that girl again, Jessica thought as she pushed away her hot-fudge sundae.

"So who's psyched for the victory barbecue at the beach?" Jessica asked, loudly enough for the whole restaurant to hear. "We have plenty to celebrate!"

"I am! I am!" different voices echoed around the room. "Party on!"

"I've got a great tape I just made of all my favorite dance songs in case anyone gets the urge to boogie down," Jessica said as she moved her arms around in the air and snapped her fingers.

"What are you doing, Jessica?" Lila asked. "Are you losing it?"

"I'm booth dancing!" Jessica announced. "It's the latest thing; in fact, it's so late that I just invented it this minute!"

Jessica was pleased to see that everyone was laughing at her joke, and once again she was the center of attention. *Back where I belong!* she thought with a smile.

Will I ever have another boyfriend? Jessica wondered as she sat alone on a blanket at the barbecue, watching the sun set over the ocean. The excitement about the game had died down, and now everyone had paired off. Maria Santelli was sitting with Winston Egbert. Elizabeth and her boyfriend, Todd Wilkins, were laughing and kissing a few yards away, and Amy Sutton and Barry Rork were strolling along the shore, holding hands. She felt as if she were the only person in the world who wasn't part of a couple.

Jessica had never had a hard time getting a boyfriend in the past. In fact, she almost always had *someone*. Her heart had been broken recently, however, and she didn't know if it would ever be whole again.

Jeremy Randall had been older and gorgeous, and she'd fallen madly in love with him the first second she'd laid eyes on him. In fact, they'd met on this exact beach. It had all seemed so magical. She'd been hit on the head with a Frisbee, and the next minute a hunky blond fantasy man with the most inviting smile she'd ever seen was looking down at her, asking her if she was all right.

But the man of her dreams had turned out to be a nightmare. Not only had he planned to hit her on the head with the Frisbee so he could get to know her, but Jessica found out that he'd only been using her to swindle a fortune out of another woman, the Wakefields' houseguest, Sue Gibbons. The thing that had hurt the most, though, was accepting the fact that all the love he'd claimed to feel for Jessica was only an act. *How will I ever be able to trust another guy again?* Jessica thought, watching the sky turn a deep red as the sun slowly slipped behind the water.

Jessica swallowed hard to make the lump in her throat go away, and she hugged her knees to her chest.

"What's a beautiful girl like you doing sitting alone watching the sunset?" Ken Matthews asked Jessica as he sat down next to her, his shoulder brushing against hers.

Jessica had been so lost in her thoughts that she practically jumped up from the blanket at the sound of Ken's voice. She pushed a strand of hair

8

out of her face and looked into Ken's eyes. *He's really handsome,* Jessica thought, feeling a slight flutter in her stomach in spite of herself. She had known Ken forever, but as she looked at him now with the glow of the sunset on his face and his shiny blond hair, it was as if she were seeing him for the first time.

Ken had been an especially good friend to her when she'd been going through the hard time with Jeremy. He had encouraged her to go out with the whole Sweet Valley gang one night—something she hadn't done since she'd met Jeremy—and one day at school, when she was feeling particularly low, he'd surprised her with a perfect white rose.

He'd even invited her to the Mistletoe Madness dance, but she hadn't been able to go, as that was the night she and Elizabeth and Sue Gibbons were laying the trap to catch Jeremy. When it was all over, and Jeremy had been arrested for fraud, it was all everybody at school was talking about. After all, Jessica had been *engaged* to him, and now he was in prison. But despite all the gossip, Ken had stayed by her side as a supportive friend.

Now she wanted to tell him how much she'd appreciated his friendship during that difficult time.

"I just wanted to say . . ." Jessica began.

9

"You know, I've been meaning to . . ." Ken said at the same time.

They both laughed awkwardly, and Jessica, feeling herself blushing, turned away.

"Let's go for a swim," Ken said, pulling Jessica up by the hand. "I'll race you to the water."

Jessica, relieved to have the tension broken, jumped up and pulled off her yellow halter sundress, revealing the new white bikini she was wearing. They ran together into the waves laughing and splashing, and Jessica couldn't remember the last time she'd felt so happy.

"That was one of the most beautiful sunsets I've ever seen," Todd said to Elizabeth as he pulled her closer to him. They were huddled together on a blanket, and the sky was almost completely dark. "I could sit like this forever, just feeling you next to me, watching the water. Are you as happy as I am?"

"Huh? Oh, yeah," Elizabeth said, distracted. She was barely listening to a word Todd was saying. Her attention was focused on the couple frolicking in the waves.

"Do you want to go to a movie tomorrow night with Maria and Winston?" Todd asked, stroking Elizabeth's long blond hair.

"Hmmm," Elizabeth muttered.

"Earth to Elizabeth!" Todd teased as he waved

his hand in front of her face. "What planet are you visiting?"

"Sorry?" Elizabeth asked, turning her gaze toward him for the first time.

"The question is, what are you *thinking* about?" Todd said. "I feel like you're a million miles away."

"Oh, I'm not thinking about anything in particular," Elizabeth lied. The truth was that Elizabeth was thinking about the sick feeling she was having in her stomach. She looked back at the water where she could still see her sister and Ken laughing and splashing each other in the fading twilight.

"So do you want to go to the movies tomorrow with Maria and Winston?" Todd asked again. "If you'd rather do something just the two of us, that would be great too." Todd kissed her left cheek. "You know I'm always happy to be alone with you."

"A movie sounds great," Elizabeth said, trying to force her attention back to Todd. "Whatever you want to do is fine with me."

As hard as she tried, Elizabeth couldn't push that sick feeling away. And she couldn't keep herself from watching Jessica and Ken in the distance.

"That felt great!" Ken said as he and Jessica emerged from the water. They were standing close together, shivering from the water. The air was getting chillier now that it was completely dark.

Jessica looked up at Ken, whose face was glowing in the moonlight. "It sure did," Jessica said, squeezing the water out of her hair. "Whew! That last wave almost knocked the breath out of me."

"Jessica," Ken started in a serious tone as he gently put one hand on her hip and then took it away. "I wanted to tell you that I . . . I think you're really terrific."

Jessica's heart raced, and it wasn't just from the waves and the cold. She was totally charmed by Ken's awkwardness and sincerity. It was so unlike Jeremy, who was always so smooth and in control.

She suddenly realized that they were in total darkness and no one sitting on the beach could see them. She stepped toward him. Their faces were so close together, they were almost touching. Ken took Jessica's face in his hands and held it tenderly as he looked deeply into her eyes. She could feel his whole body tremble as he moved even closer to her and kissed her on the lips.

"What's going on?" Elizabeth asked Todd. She had been lying on her back looking for constellations, trying to distract herself from thoughts of Ken and Jessica cavorting in the waves, when suddenly there was a commotion on the beach. People were laughing and cheering.

"It's just Bruce showing off the spotlights on his father's new Jeep," Todd said, lifting himself up on one elbow. Bruce usually cruised around in his own black Porsche, but his father had just gotten a new Jeep Cherokee that Bruce had driven down to the beach.

There were more cheers and catcalls, and Todd and Elizabeth stood up to see what all the excitement was about. The Jeep's spotlights, which were incredibly powerful, were shining on a couple deeply engrossed in a kiss.

"Isn't that your sister with Ken?" Todd asked Elizabeth.

"It couldn't be," Elizabeth said, hearing her own voice shaking.

"Take another look," Todd said, laughing. "It looks like there's a new couple on the horizon."

Elizabeth squinted. *It can't be*, she thought in desperation. Laughing and splashing in the waves was one thing, but *kissing*? Jessica and Ken?

Everyone on the beach started clapping for the couple. Everyone except Elizabeth.

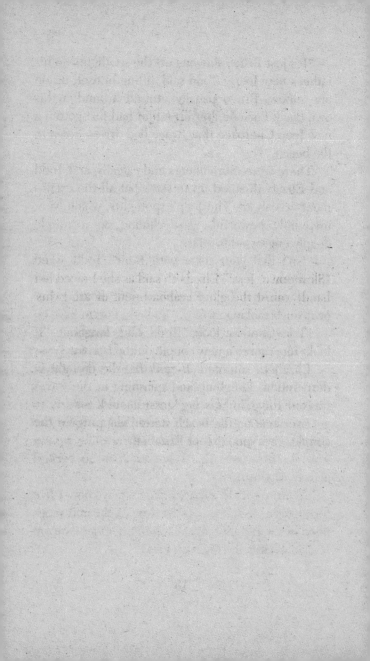

Chapter 2

"Slow down, Jess!" Elizabeth said as she braced her hand against the glove compartment of the twins' Jeep on Monday morning. "You're going to have an accident if you don't stop driving like a lunatic."

"Stop worrying so much. It's bad for your health," Jessica said as she whirled around a corner. "You know I'm an expert driver."

"Since when have you been in such a hurry to get to school?" Usually Elizabeth had to force her sister to get out of bed, but that morning Jessica was the first one up. "What are you so excited about? Algebra class?"

"Yeah, right." Jessica laughed. "You know I live for algebra." She stopped at a red light and reapplied her matte pink lipstick in the rearview mirror.

"So what *is* the big rush for?"

"I'm just anxious to get to school because I know everyone's going to still be buzzing about the awesome job we cheerleaders did on Friday, thanks to me, of course," Jessica said excitedly, flooring the gas pedal when the light turned green. "And second of all, I'm looking forward to seeing Ken."

Elizabeth looked out the window at the houses and trees that were whizzing past, so Jessica wouldn't be able to see the pained expression on her face. She wished she could tell her sister what she was feeling, but that was impossible. She couldn't tell her, because Jessica didn't know that she had had a fling with Ken when Todd had moved to Vermont for a brief period earlier that year. Nobody in the entire world knew except Elizabeth and Ken.

Todd and Ken were best friends, and when Todd was away, he had asked Ken to keep an eye on Elizabeth. They had spent a lot of time together, and at first they were just good friends. After all, they had known each other forever. They could talk for hours on end about anything, and they had so much in common.

But eventually they realized that their feelings for each other were more than just friendly. Elizabeth had tried to push away her romantic feelings, out of loyalty to Todd, but soon she was overcome by her attraction to Ken. When he had finally kissed her, she hadn't been able to resist him, and they dated on the sly for a couple of weeks.

Finally, though, they had decided to end the relationship before anyone—namely, Todd—got hurt. The guilt they had felt over deceiving him was destroying them both, and they knew it couldn't go on. When Todd had come back to Sweet Valley, their relationship had already been over for a long time, and she and Ken had gone back to the way they had always been, just friends. They promised each other never to tell anyone about what had happened while Todd was gone. But because they'd broken off the relationship so quickly—before it had had a chance to cool down naturally—it hadn't really come to a natural end, and now Elizabeth was worried. *Maybe I still have feelings for Ken*, Elizabeth thought as she looked over at her sister's radiant face.

Elizabeth knew better than anyone how horrible it had been for Jessica when Jeremy had turned out to be nothing more than a callous criminal, and she wanted to be happy about her sister's new romantic interest—but why did it have to be Ken? The idea of the two of them together drove Elizabeth crazy. *Maybe that kiss they shared on the beach was a fluke,* Elizabeth hoped. *Maybe it will all blow over....*

Where is everyone? Jessica wondered as she stood by her locker later that morning. She had been taking her time hanging out in the hallway before going to her first class, wanting to give people a chance to shower her with praise about Friday's game. Normally, her friends swarmed around her on Mondays before first period, eager to talk about the weekend, but nobody seemed to be around. *That's strange*, she thought as she brushed her hair before the little mirror that hung on the inside of her locker door.

That morning when she'd gotten dressed, she'd been thinking of Ken and had wanted to look her very best for him. She'd decided on her favorite— faded blue jeans and her blue-and-gold gauzy blouse that looked as if it were from the sixties. For a minute she had wondered if it was her style, but then she'd decided that since she'd seen blouses like it in all the fashion magazines, it was just right. Besides, blue was a great color on her, and she knew she looked beautiful.

She couldn't wait to see Ken again after they'd kissed on Friday night. All weekend she'd played that moment in the moonlight over and over in her head. Just when she'd been about to give up on romance and guys, she mused, Ken had come along with his gorgeous smile and had swept her away.

Just then she heard a buzz of voices down the hallway. She looked toward the commotion and caught a glimpse of Ken at the end of the hall. He was standing in a big crowd of people who were swarming around someone or something. At that moment Lila spotted Jessica and, breaking free from the crowd, met her at her locker. "Did you see her yet?"

"Did I see who yet?" Jessica asked, flipping her hair over her head and then letting it fall back into place to give it more volume. Now that she'd spotted Ken, she wanted to look as good as possible.

"Heather Mallone," Lila said, pointing down the hall to the crowd of people. "That girl at the Dairi Burger on Friday who caused such a big hoopla with the guys."

"What about her?" Jessica said, slamming her locker door. She knew she wasn't going to like whatever Lila was about to tell her, and she already felt the great mood she'd been in that morning start to fade away.

"Well, that's her down there," Lila said. "She just moved to Sweet Valley, and she's a student here now. You should see the way the guys are flirting their heads off with her."

"And that's headline news?" Jessica said, trying to sound casual.

"Well," Lila said. "I have a feeling she's going to be pretty popular, judging from the reaction she's getting after being here just a few minutes."

"Whoop-dee-doo," Jessica said, twirling her finger in the air. "Let's call the local television station

19

and tell them the big scoop—a new girl has arrived in Sweet Valley. I mean, who cares?"

"I do. She seems like someone we might want to know. She seems like our type. Oh, and by the way," Lila added casually, looking closely at Jessica, "I think I heard her saying something about being a big deal on her old cheerleading squad."

Jessica knew her best friend well enough to know that Lila was just trying to get a rise out of her.

"As I said in the Dairi Burger," Jessica replied, doing her best to smile, "I don't see what the fuss is about. 'Big deal' is a relative term, and besides, she's probably got some major personality flaw."

"How can you possibly know that?" Lila asked as she adjusted the tight purple minidress she was wearing. "You haven't even met her yet. I think I just might detect a note of jealousy."

"Be real," Jessica said, rolling her eyes. "I can tell things about people from just looking at them." *And major personality flaw or not, I can tell that I don't like anything about this girl,* Jessica thought, mad that for the second time in a row this Heather Mallone had stolen her thunder.

"Here she comes," Lila said.

Jessica turned to watch Heather and a sea of people walk down the hall toward her. She scanned the crowd for Ken, but he wasn't there. Her heart sank for a moment, and then her gaze landed on

Heather, who was beaming at her with what Jessica knew was a phony smile.

"Lila, you know Heather, right?" Annie asked.

"Well, we just met a little while ago in the parking lot," Lila said, extending her hand to meet Heather's. "But we weren't properly introduced. I'm Lila Fowler."

"Hi, I'm Heather Mallone. Thanks again for letting me have that parking space."

"No problem," Lila said. "That's a great car you have, by the way. It's totally cool."

Jessica couldn't believe how Lila was kissing up to her. And she let her have her parking space?

"Thanks," Heather said. "I'd be happy to take you riding in it sometime. I'm still unfamiliar with Sweet Valley, and I could use a good tour guide."

"That would be great," Lila said.

I'll be your tour guide, Jessica thought, *I'll show you the way right out of town.*

"This is Jessica Wakefield," Lila said, pushing Jessica forward.

"Hi, Jessica," Heather said, smiling that same syrupy smile as she extended her hand to Jessica. "What an adorable little blouse you're wearing. It's so, uh . . . retro."

"Retro?" Jessica repeated, not knowing exactly what Heather meant, but pretty sure it wasn't a compliment. *I knew I wasn't going to like this*

21

person, Jessica thought as she scrutinized the girl standing in front of her.

Heather had long blond hair that was wavy and curly and hung in layers around her face. She had big blue eyes and a dainty little nose, and as much as Jessica hated to admit it to herself—she *was* beautiful. She was wearing skintight designer blue jeans that showed off a muscular but thin figure, and a white silk blouse that looked tailored and elegant. She had on expensive-looking black loafers with no socks. And her jewelry, which consisted of gold earrings, a gold bracelet, and a gold choker, were from a line Jessica recognized from one of the most exclusive jewelry catalogs she'd seen at Lila's house.

Jessica suddenly knew what Lila had meant when she'd said that Heather was "our type." *She really meant that Heather was her type, as in super-rich!* Lila herself was the richest girl in Sweet Valley. Although Jessica loved to hang out in the sprawling mansion where she lived with her parents, she couldn't help being jealous of all her money and her ability to buy whatever she wanted whenever she wanted it.

"Yeah, you know, 'retro,' like from the sixties," Heather explained authoritatively. "That look is very trendy these days."

Jessica looked at Lila, then at Annie in disbelief. She was waiting for them to acknowledge the fact that Heather was insulting her, but nobody else seemed to notice. *Not only is she a fake, but she's condescending and rude,* Jessica thought.

"Excuse me, but I have to get to class," Jessica said as she turned and stormed off. In just a few minutes Jessica's mood had taken a nosedive, and it was all because of one person: Heather Mallone. *The less I see of that girl, the better,* Jessica thought as she walked down the hall, leaving behind Heather and her group of adoring fans.

"Can you believe what a phony that new girl is?" Jessica asked her group of friends at the lunch table later that day. "I couldn't believe how rude she was to me this morning."

"Oh, please, Jessica," Lila said. "She was perfectly nice. In fact, I think I'm going to like her a lot."

Jessica's mouth dropped open incredulously. "She totally trashed my blouse this morning in front of everyone. You were standing right there when she did it."

"I think you're being paranoid," Lila said as she poured two packets of sugar into her iced tea. "She was complimenting you."

"Excuse me, but since when is 'trendy' considered a compliment?" Jessica asked. She couldn't believe that her best friend didn't even see how awful Heather was.

"Hey, guys," Annie said brightly as she set down her tray at the table. "Look who's joining us for lunch."

Jessica looked up from her plate of fettuccine Alfredo and almost dropped her fork. Heather plopped herself down at their table and sat directly across from Jessica. She had that same fake smile plastered on her face that she'd had that morning. *My lunch is ruined,* Jessica thought.

"So how do you like Sweet Valley High so far?" Amy asked. "Are you finding your way around OK?"

"It's fabulous," Heather said. "Everyone's so nice and friendly here."

"Especially the guys," Annie said, giggling. "You should see the way every male in this school has offered to show Heather around. She already had five guys ask her out for this weekend."

Jessica's dislike for Heather was mounting with every minute.

"I have to say, though, that the guys seem pretty immature here," Heather said.

This is just too much, Jessica thought. *Now she's insulting the guys in our school!* Jessica looked around the table to see if anyone else was bothered by Heather's rude comment, but nobody even seemed to notice.

"You're right about that," Lila agreed. "They're totally unsophisticated. Look at that table over there

24

by the window. Every single day those guys are over there playing paper football. Talk about childish."

Jessica looked over at Aaron Dallas, Ronnie Edwards, and the other guys Lila was referring to. They did look pretty ridiculous the way they were so engrossed in their game, making a lot of silly cheering noises over a little piece of paper being flicked from one end of the table to the other. Still, they were Sweet Valley guys, and she suddenly felt very loyal to them.

Everyone burst out laughing at Lila's observation, except Jessica. *How can Lila agree with her like that?* she wondered. *What a traitor. She's just agreeing with Heather because she thinks she's cool, and rich.*

"That pasta you're eating is loaded with fat," Heather said, pointing to Jessica's plate.

"So?" Jessica said, looking up from her lunch defensively.

"Fat clogs up your arteries and causes heart attacks. I've completely eliminated fat from my diet. If I ate like that, I'd never be able to fit into my jeans."

"Well, I can understand that, judging from the kind of jeans you like to wear," Jessica said, trying to make her voice light.

"What do you mean?" Heather asked.

"Oh, I just mean that you obviously like to wear

your jeans really, really tight," Jessica said. "I'm surprised you can even walk in them. How long does it take you to put them on in the morning? I'd imagine you'd have to have a crew of people pulling them up for you."

Jessica looked around the table expecting to see her friends giggle in agreement, but everyone just stared at Jessica as if she had leprosy or something.

Heather smiled at Jessica, ignoring her comments. "I just don't know any girls my age who eat food like that anymore. Everyone I know watches their weight."

She looked at Heather's plate, which was full of carrot and celery sticks and some tuna without a trace of mayonnaise. "Well, I guess I'm just one of those lucky people who don't have to worry about their weight," Jessica said, wrapping a huge helping of fettuccine around her fork. "I don't believe in depriving myself of anything."

"You do have a great figure, Heather," Maria gushed. "You look like you exercise a lot."

"I guess you could say I'm pretty athletic," Heather said as she chomped on a carrot stick. "I jog five miles every morning before school, and I play a lot of squash and tennis. Oh, and I'm an avid skier."

"Really? Where do you go?" Lila asked.

"Aspen, naturally, and every Christmas my family goes to Gstaad," Heather said, as if everyone knew where she was talking about.

"I love Gstaad," Lila said, "especially the boutiques there."

"Shtad?" Jessica asked. "It sounds like some kind of sausage or something."

Lila and Heather looked at each other and laughed.

"It's a very exclusive ski resort in Switzerland," Heather explained as if she were talking to a child.

"Don't you remember when my dad and I went there a few years ago?" Lila asked, sipping from her iced tea. "I'm sure I sent you a postcard."

"Gee, I guess I forgot. I'll have to go home and dust off my collection of postcards from Lila's travels," Jessica said sarcastically, furious that Lila was siding with Heather.

"Well, I can't imagine doing as much exercise as you do, Heather," Amy said. "You must be exhausted at the end of every day."

"It helps keep me in shape for cheerleading," Heather said before chomping on a carrot stick.

"Heather was just telling me that the cheerleading squad at her old school were the state champions of Nevada for seven years," Annie gushed. "And she was the captain!"

"Wow, that's great," Maria said. "You must be a really wonderful cheerleader."

27

"I understand that you're one of the captains of the squad here," Heather said to Jessica. "What kind of stuff are you into?"

"Well, I make up most of the cheers myself, but sometimes I use *Cheerleading* magazine for inspiration," Jessica said, proud that she had the vision as a captain to keep up with the latest moves. "You should have seen us on Friday. We were awesome." Jessica waited for her friends to agree with her, but nobody did. They were all too focused on Heather.

"*Cheerleading* magazine?" Heather laughed. "That's so *dated*. If I were you, Jessica, I wouldn't waste my money on a subscription. Don't you watch VTV? Hip-hop's the latest thing in cheerleading," Heather said knowingly.

"I guess our cheers would seem pretty boring to you," Robin said. "They're not that exciting, nothing like VTV."

Not that exciting! Jessica was mortified. She had worked on those cheers for weeks, and now her very own cocaptain was putting them down in front of this awful, show-off Heather! Just when she thought she wasn't going to be able to take it anymore, Jessica saw that Ken was walking toward their table.

"Who's that? I noticed him this morning. He's one of the cutest guys I've seen all day," Heather said, sitting up and running ran her fingers through her hair.

"That's Ken Matthews," Lila said, looking warily at Jessica. "He's the quarterback of the football team, and he threw the winning pass on Friday."

If he's coming over here to talk to Heather I'm going to have to throw my fettuccine in her face, Jessica thought as she watched Ken's gaze closely to see if he was checking Heather out. To her delight he didn't even glance at Heather. Instead, he walked right over to Jessica and leaned down to her from behind her chair.

"Hey, Jessica, do you want to come over and sit with me?" Ken asked timidly but sweetly.

"I'd love to eat lunch with you, Ken," Jessica said loudly as she stood up and picked up her tray.

To Jessica's dismay Heather and Jessica's friends barely even noticed that Jessica was leaving the table with Ken. Heather was going on about how great her cheerleaders were at her old school.

They're too busy falling all over Heather to notice me, Jessica thought as she followed Ken to his table.

"I really had a good time on Friday night," Ken said to Jessica, putting his tray down at an empty table. "I hope that you weren't too embarrassed when everyone saw us kissing like that."

"I had a great time too," Jessica said. "And I wasn't embarrassed at all."

Jessica looked back over at her table of friends and was pleased to see that finally she was getting some attention. They were all obviously talking about her and Ken, because they kept looking in Jessica's direction. Most important, Heather was watching them with particular interest.

Ken looked down at his plate and moved his fettucine around nervously. Finally, after what seemed like an eternity of silence, Ken spoke.

"Jessica, I was wondering if you'd consider going out with me on Friday night," he said, avoiding eye contact with her. "I mean, if you don't want to, that's fine too. I just thought it might be fun, you know, to do something together."

Jessica was thrilled beyond belief. "I'd love to!"

"You would?" Ken asked incredulously, looking into her eyes for the first time since they'd sat down. "Well, then it's a date."

Chapter 3

Elizabeth was going over "Personal Profiles," the column she wrote for *The Oracle*, on Monday afternoon. Todd was sitting across from her in the newspaper office waiting for her to finish, and she was getting slightly annoyed by his constant talking and joking around. Usually she welcomed his playful moods, but today he was getting on her nerves.

"Aren't you ready yet?" Todd asked impatiently as he threw the tenth piece of crumpled paper into the wastebasket. Each time he threw one in successfully, he clapped his hands and said, "Two points!"

"I'm just trying to get this column finished," Elizabeth said. *And I'm having a hard time doing it because of that annoying game you keep playing with yourself,* she wanted to say.

"You've gone over that column a hundred times."

31

"I just keep trying to think of something else to put in it to give it a little more life. This has got to be the most boring column I've ever written," Elizabeth complained. "The profile of a new chess-team member is not my idea of juicy."

"I have something that will spice up your column," Todd said with a big smile. "The profile of two people starting a new romance."

"Really?" Elizabeth looked up from her notebook. "Who is it? I'm desperate for anything."

"I'll give you a hint—they're both really popular . . ." Todd said.

"Are you going to tell me, or do I have to guess?" Elizabeth said, unable to mask her impatience.

"You have to guess," Todd said playfully. "One of them is a cheerleader, and one of them is a football player, and they're both really good-looking."

"That could be a lot of people," Elizabeth said, afraid of what—or who—Todd was getting at.

"You're not very good at guessing games," Todd said. "It's Jessica and Ken!"

Even though Elizabeth had known that's who Todd had been talking about, her heart sank. Careful not to let Todd see her disappointment, she asked simply, "What makes you think they're a couple? One little kiss doesn't constitute a relationship."

"But a date for this coming Friday does," Todd said.

"How do you know they're going on a date?" Elizabeth asked, trying to sound nonchalant.

"Ken just told me he asked your sister out during lunch today," Todd said, flipping a pencil in the air. "He's really excited about it. It seems like he's into Jessica in a big way."

Todd's words cut like a knife through Elizabeth's heart. "They've been friends forever," she said. "Maybe he just asked her out as a friend." Elizabeth was desperately trying to convince herself that it wasn't anything more than just a simple, friendly date.

"I guess it's like that movie we saw together about those people who were friends for years, then suddenly they realized they were in love," Todd said. "I think it's great. As you know, I've never been the biggest fan of your sister's, but I think she could be good for Ken. And I'm happy for him. It's great to see him so excited about somebody. They'd make a great couple. Don't you think?"

"Oh, yeah, they'd be perfect together," Elizabeth lied.

Todd leaned across the table. "Just like we are," he said before he kissed Elizabeth tenderly on the mouth.

Elizabeth closed her eyes and kissed Todd

back. But instead of kissing Todd with all her heart, she was remembering her kisses with Ken. Horrified, she opened her eyes. *I'm kissing Todd and thinking of Ken! I'm a terrible person!*

The cheerleaders were stretching on the far end of the football field when Jessica arrived at practice that afternoon. Jessica was excited to start teaching a new cheer she'd worked on all weekend. She quickly read it over and couldn't wait to share it with the girls.

She dropped her notebook onto the ground, feeling proud of the great new words, and ran in front of the waiting squad.

"OK, girls," Jessica said loudly. "You all did a fantastic job on Friday, and I'm not the only one who thinks so. The crowds loved us and we were better than ever. We can't rest on laurels, though, so I want you to pay close attention to the new routine I'm about to show you."

When Jessica had finished talking, she realized that most of the girls were looking at something behind her. She turned around and saw Heather standing with her hands on her hips and a smirk on her face.

"May I help you?" Jessica asked, unable to keep the annoyance out of her voice.

"Yeah, as a matter of fact you can," Heather

said. "I want to try out for the squad."

Over my dead body, Jessica wanted to say. But instead she cleared her throat and said sweetly, "Well, then, you can come back in the spring and try out with the other seventy-five or so girls who want to be on our squad. Why don't you run along home now and practice, and come back next season?"

Jessica turned back toward the girls and raised her arms to start the first cheer.

"Wait, Jessica!" Robin shouted. "I asked Heather to come to practice. I thought that we could really benefit from her expertise, so I invited her to try out. I know it's not really the usual time of year that we audition new people, but I thought we could make an exception since she was the captain of a champion team at her old school."

Jessica could hardly believe her ears. Now she had no choice. Robin was her cocaptain, and if Jessica made a big stink about Heather trying out, everyone would think she was jealous. "Fine, Heather can try out," Jessica said. *But she's going to wish she never came to practice today after I'm through with her.* "I want you to do a triple herky, a back flip, a Y-leap combination, a no-hands cartwheel, and a landing jump in the splits. Oh, and you'll need to do that in under three minutes."

"No problem," Heather said nonchalantly. "Do you have a watch to time me with?"

"Yes, I do," Jessica said. "On your mark—get set—go!"

Jessica sat down with the other girls and, much to her dismay, watched Heather complete the routine in two minutes. Not only did she do everything Jessica said, but she added complicated, funky dance steps between each move. When she finished, she gave Jessica one of her sickeningly sweet smiles. Jessica had never seen anyone do such a complicated routine with such expertise and grace, and her head was starting to pound.

Everyone stood up to applaud and cheer, and Jessica was desperate. "Sorry, but that was over three minutes," she lied. "OK, we've wasted enough time, girls. Let's get down to business."

"Jessica, that was two minutes," Robin protested. "I timed it with my new stopwatch."

"It must not be working," Jessica said dismissively.

"My watch said two minutes, too," said Annie.

"So did mine," Helen said.

"Well, I guess I'll have to get my watch fixed." Jessica was flustered, and she felt her face turning red. She looked at Heather, who was as cool as a cucumber. She wasn't even sweating or breathing heavily after that strenuous routine.

"So I think that does it," Robin said. "It looks like we have a new member on the squad."

"Not so fast," Jessica said over the cheers coming from the girls. "We have to take a vote on it."

"Judging from the reaction of the entire squad, I would say that Heather's a shoo-in," Robin said, "and I think it's a waste of time to even take a vote on it. Everyone seems to love her."

"We still have to vote. And we need to do it in private." She turned to Heather and gave her back one of her syrupy smiles. "So maybe you could leave now."

"Sure thing," Heather said, smiling back and turning on her heel.

"'Bye, Heather!" the girls chanted as if she were God's gift to cheerleading.

"See ya later," Heather said sweetly, looking over her shoulder. "Have a good practice!"

Heather walked off the field and into the parking lot, where she got into her covertible and drove off.

Have a good practice! Jessica didn't think she'd ever disliked anyone as much as she disliked Heather Mallone. And if she had anything to do about it, Heather would never be on her cheering squad.

"She was awesome," Amy gushed. "She made it all look so effortless."

37

"And she made a normal routine look like a fun dance," Robin said. "She really jazzed up our usual moves."

"I don't think we even need to vote," Jeannie said. "We obviously all loved her."

"We have to take a vote," Jessica said, wondering how she was going to manage keeping Heather off the squad. "It's standard procedure."

"OK, all those in favor of Heather joining our squad, raise their right hand," Robin said.

Everyone raised their hand except Jessica. *Think of something, think of something,* she told herself.

"That settles it," Robin said. "Sorry, Jessica, but majority rules."

"No, in this case we have to discuss it further," Jessica said. "Just because she's a good cheerleader doesn't mean she's right for our squad."

"What are you talking about?" Robin asked. "Isn't that what we care about? Someone who can do all the routines?"

"We have to think about the personality and character of everyone on our team," Jessica said. "Everyone in this school looks up to us. We have a reputation to live up to. We can't let just anyone on our team just because they can do a cart-wheel."

"Jessica, you have to admit she did a lot more

than just a cartwheel out there," Robin said. "If there were an Olympics category for cheerleading, she'd have a gold medal."

"And besides that, think about how much we could all learn from her," Annie said. "She could really liven things up a bit. Not that we're not fabulous already, but we could be even better."

"I just think it's important not to be too hasty about this decision," Jessica said, grasping at straws.

"So what do you propose?" Robin asked.

"As cocaptain, I'm going to come up with a series of tests that she has to pass before we can accept her on the squad," Jessica said.

"What kind of tests?" Jeannie asked. "Cheerleading tests? Written tests?"

"Tests that demonstrate her strength of character," Jessica said. "I'm going to think about them tonight when I go home, and we can start the testing process tomorrow."

"It seems sort of silly after her performance today," Robin said.

"Well, I *am* the cocaptain, so I guess you'll all just have to go along with what I say," Jessica said, jumping up from the circle. *And I'm going to have to come up with tests that she'll never be able to pass! I don't care if she has to walk across a bed of nails—she's not going to be on this squad!*

Elizabeth sat on her bed before dinner that night trying to concentrate on the book she was reading for American-history class about the labor movement in the thirties. She kept reading the same paragraph over and over again. All she could think about was the kiss she'd shared with Todd earlier that day. *What does it mean if I'm kissing Todd and thinking of Ken?* she worried. *I must still have feelings for Ken!*

She loved Todd, but she couldn't stop thinking about Ken. Was it possible to love two people at the same time?

"Hey, Liz, I have the best news," Jessica said as she came flying through the door.

"Does the word 'knock' mean anything to you?" Elizabeth was startled out of her thoughts, suddenly afraid that her sister would be able to read her mind. "I *was* trying to study."

"Grouchy, grouchy, grouchy," Jessica teased as she plopped down onto Elizabeth's bed. "It's been medically proved that too much studying is bad for your health." Jessica grabbed Elizabeth's book and flung it onto the floor.

"Now you made me lose my place," Elizabeth said, picking up her book.

"So guess who I have a date with on Friday night?" Jessica asked, grinning ear to ear.

"Ken Matthews," Elizabeth said unexcitedly.

"How do you know?"

"Todd told me today. I guess Ken told him."

"Isn't it fantastic? He's the greatest, cutest guy, and he's always been such a good friend."

"Yeah, it's great," Elizabeth forced herself to say.

"You don't seem too excited for me," Jessica said.

"I just think you should take it slowly," Elizabeth said, hating herself for putting a damper on Jessica's happiness. "It wasn't so long ago that you had your heart broken by Jeremy, don't forget."

"How could I ever forget what he did to me?" Jessica asked, looking melancholy for a moment and then perking right up again. "That's exactly why I'm so happy about Ken. I thought I'd never be interested in another guy ever again after Jeremy."

"All I'm saying is be careful," Elizabeth cautioned.

"Ken is nothing like Jeremy," Jessica swooned. "He's so natural and unpretentious, and I can tell he really likes me."

"How can you be so sure?" Elizabeth asked, hating herself for making her sister doubt Ken's feelings for her, but not being able to stop.

"I can tell from the way he kissed me on

Friday," Jessica said. "He was so tender but passionate at the same time. I felt his whole body trembling when he was standing next to me. Our attraction to each other was overwhelming."

As Jessica described her kiss with Ken, Elizabeth remembered her own secret kisses with him. Her entire body felt heavy with sadness and longing for something magical in the past. Magical yet fleeting, she thought.

"Kissing can be deceiving," Elizabeth said in spite of herself. "Just because two people like to kiss each other doesn't mean they should be together in a relationship."

"But before we ever even kissed, he acted like such a loyal friend to me when most of my supposed friends were just gossiping about me. I feel like he knows me in a way Jeremy never even began to know me. I've never felt this way about a guy before. It's like the perfect combination—friendship and romance."

"I wish I had a dollar for every time you've said you never felt that way about a guy before," Elizabeth said. "I'd be a millionaire. You've fallen in love more times than I can even remember."

"But this time is different," Jessica said. "I really feel like we were meant to be together. I think this could develop into a really serious relationship."

"I think you should still date around," Elizabeth said, though she could hardly believe she was saying it. "It's never a good idea to go from one relationship to another without checking out the other fish in the sea for a while."

Jessica laughed. "That's really funny, coming from you," Jessica said. "I've never seen you date around."

Yeah, well, you'd be surprised, Elizabeth thought, but then continued, "You're totally on the rebound. It's easy to think you're falling for someone new after being hurt the way you were. In a week or two you'll probably just want to be friends with Ken."

"I promise you you're wrong," Jessica said. "And I wish you'd be a little happier for me. I'm going to go get ready for dinner. Mom said it's almost ready."

Elizabeth felt like a rotten sister. She knew how important it was for Jessica to be with somebody new. *Maybe* I'm *in love with Ken,* Elizabeth thought. *Why else would I be trying to take away my sister's happiness?*

Chapter 4

Elizabeth hesitated by the door of Mr. Collins's office on Tuesday morning, trying to decide whether or not to knock. Mr. Collins was the faculty adviser to *The Oracle*, and Elizabeth had gone to him on many occasions to ask his advice. She needed to talk to someone more than ever, and she didn't want to talk to her best friend Enid Rollins or any of her other friends about it, because she was afraid of what they'd think of her.

When she'd woken up that morning, she'd felt an overwhelming sense of doom. Her first thought of the day had been about Jessica and Ken and the date they were going to have on Friday. She felt so alone in her feelings of guilt and jealousy. The two people she felt the closest to in the world—Jessica and Todd—were the two people she couldn't talk to about her problem, because it was about them.

Maybe it's a bad idea to talk to Mr. Collins about it, Elizabeth decided as she turned to walk away.

Just as Elizabeth took two steps away from his office, Mr. Collins opened his door and peeked into the hallway.

"Good morning, Ms. Wakefield," Mr. Collins said happily. "What brings you here so early? Problems with this week's issue of *The Oracle*?"

"Well, I do have a problem, but it has nothing to do with journalism," Elizabeth said. "Actually, it's a problem, umm . . . a friend of mine is having. I can come back another time, though, if you're busy."

"You know I'm never too busy to talk to you," Mr. Collins said as he led Elizabeth into his office. "What's on your mind?"

"Do you mind if we shut the door?" Elizabeth asked. She didn't want to run the risk of someone walking by and overhearing her. It was hard to keep anything a secret at Sweet Valley High—especially the kind of thing Elizabeth was about to tell Mr. Collins.

"This sounds serious," Mr. Collins said as he stood back up to close the door, looking concerned. "What kind of problem is your friend having?"

"It's a relationship problem," Elizabeth started awkwardly. "A few months ago my friend's boyfriend was out of town for a few months. Well, while he was gone, she had a sort-of fling with his best friend."

"I see," Mr. Collins said thoughtfully. "And did your friend tell her boyfriend about it when he came back to town?"

"No, she didn't tell anyone about it," Elizabeth said, feeling those guilty emotions creep back. "The problem now is that somebody else, someone who's really, really close to my friend, is starting a relationship with this same guy."

"And this is making your friend feel jealous," Mr. Collins said.

"Exactly!" Elizabeth said. It was amazing to her that Mr. Collins was always able to understand a situation without her having to explain it. He was wiser than almost anyone Elizabeth knew. "She didn't realize she still had feelings for this person until he started dating someone else."

"It sounds like things between your friend and this person she was secretly seeing never really got resolved," Mr. Collins said.

"You're right," Elizabeth said. "Before my friend's boyfriend came back to town, she'd stopped seeing the other guy. They both agreed that it wasn't right to keep seeing each other. But since things ended, they never really had another conversation about everything that had happened between them. My friend felt so guilty about betraying her boyfriend that she tried to push it all away—pretend like it never happened."

"But seeing him with someone else makes that difficult," Mr. Collins said, reading her mind again.

"Yes, it's unbearable," Elizabeth said, and then quickly added, "for my friend. It's unbearable for my friend."

"Obviously your friend hasn't resolved her feelings for this other person. Until she does, she's going to be miserable."

"I know you're right, but it's going to be hard for her," Elizabeth said sadly. *Everything he's saying makes sense, but I'm afraid I'm just going to have to swallow my feelings,* Elizabeth thought. "Thanks, Mr. Collins. I guess I should get going now."

"Are you sure that's all? I don't think I was much of a help," Mr. Collins said.

"No, you were a great help, as always," Elizabeth said. *But how am I supposed to resolve my feelings when I'm going out with Todd?*

"Heather, before I tell you what the first test is," Jessica said, "I just want to let you know that I totally understand if you want to back out of this whole cheerleading idea. I mean, it's going to be pretty strenuous, so you might want to just forget about it."

"I wouldn't dream of it," Heather said. "I can't wait to start the first test."

The girls were sitting with some of the cheerleaders and Lila at lunch on Tuesday, and the cafeteria seemed louder than usual. Jessica had intentionally chosen a big juicy hamburger and a large order of french fries from the lunch counter to show Heather she wasn't about to start counting fat grams just because she did.

Jessica took a big bite of her burger and put it back down on her plate. "OK, the first test is designed to see if you have the kind of self-confidence that's required to be on our squad. In order to measure your confidence level, you'll have to sit with the chess team during lunch for two days in a row."

"That's cruel and unusual punishment," Lila said. "They're the biggest nerds in the entire school."

"I don't know if even cheerleading is worth going through that humiliation," Robin said.

"Yeah, how is that a test of her self-confidence?" Annie asked. "I don't get it."

"Most people wouldn't be caught dead sitting with those guys," Jessica pointed out. "But if a person's really secure with herself, she won't care who she's seen sitting with. Also, it's important that as a cheerleader, she's able to get along with all kinds of people."

"When was the last time you sat with the chess team?" Lila teased. "I haven't exactly seen you being all buddy-buddy with Sean Lowry."

Jessica glared at her friend. "Maybe I have friends you don't know about."

"I don't think sitting with the chess team should be too difficult," Heather said, not skipping a beat.

"You could run the risk of damaging your reputation early on," Jessica warned. "After all, you're new in school. You don't want everyone to think you're a geek."

"I'm secure enough with myself that I don't care who I'm seen eating lunch with," Heather said as she stood up from the table and picked up her tray. "In fact, at my school in Nevada I got along with everyone. I'm going to start my test right now. I'll see you guys later."

Jessica watched aghast as Heather swaggered across the room and sat down with the startled chess team—smiling all the way.

"What's Heather wearing?" Lila asked Jessica on Wednesday morning. "She looks like a construction worker or something!"

Jessica stood calmly at her locker and looked down the hallway where Heather was obviously the laughingstock of the school. A group was formed around her, and Jessica was sure people were making fun of her clothes. *Good. My plan seems to be working perfectly,* Jessica thought triumphantly.

She had called Heather the night before and told her she had to wear whatever Jessica brought in for her the next morning. She'd rummaged through the garage and found a pair of purple-and-green-striped overalls her father had worn in a play when he was in college. She brought the overalls and a big orange cowboy hat to school and told Heather she had to put them on and wear them all day.

"It's one of the cheerleading tests I came up with," Jessica said proudly.

"You mean *you're* responsible for the way Heather looks today?" Lila asked incredulously.

"Yes, I take full responsibility. It's her second test."

"And what exactly are you testing? Her bad taste?" Lila looked back over at Heather and shook her head.

"It's a test of her depth."

"What's that supposed to mean?" Lila asked cynically.

"She seems like someone who's totally superficial, the way she's so obsessed with her looks and everything," Jessica explained. "I wanted to see if there was more to her than just her concern about her appearance."

"As if *you're* not interested in your own looks?" Lila asked, laughing. "I never knew that was one of the criteria for being on the squad."

"Well, I guess you wouldn't know because you're *not* on the squad," Jessica quipped.

"I can't believe she went along with it," Lila said. "How did you ever get her to do it?"

"She's desperate to cheer, but I'm sure that within the hour she'll be changing back into her usual clothes," Jessica said with an impish grin. "I must admit that this is one of my more clever schemes."

"It is pretty harsh," Lila said, readjusting the headband that was holding back her long brown hair. "I'm glad I'm not trying to be a cheerleader. She looks like a clown."

"Let's go hear some of the mean things people are saying to her," Jessica said, grabbing the books she needed for her first class.

Jessica and Lila walked down the hall together, and Jessica was pleased to see everyone laughing. What didn't please her was seeing that Heather was laughing as well.

"You really look cool," Bruce Patman was saying to Heather. "You're really pulling off that grunge look that's so in style these days."

"It's true," Amy agreed. "The models are wearing that stuff in all the fashion magazines I've seen recently."

"Yeah, you're on the cutting edge," Rick Hunter said. "Most girls would be too afraid to wear stuff like that. I think it's a sign of confidence that you're wearing whatever you feel like wearing."

"I agree," Sean Lowry, a member of the chess team, said. "You look really terrific."

"Thanks, Sean," Heather said, as if he were a close friend. "Oh, and that was fun last night when we worked on our math homework together."

She's hanging out with the chess team now? Jessica thought in total shock.

"How did you ever come up with this great outfit?" Annie asked.

"I have Jessica to thank," Heather said, turning to Jessica and smiling brightly in her direction.

"Don't thank me yet," Jessica said to Heather. "It's only the morning. It might get harder going around like that all day long."

"I doubt it," Heather said, walking off with Bruce. "Toodles!"

I'd like to "toodle" you, Jessica thought as she watched Heather swagger down the hall. *I have to think of another test before tomorrow, when we're supposed to vote again. But this time I'll make sure it'll be something she'll never pass.*

It was Thursday morning, and Jessica had arrived early at school. She was waiting for the students to file into the classroom for homeroom. The third and last test for Heather was about to happen, and Jessica couldn't wait to see Heather fail.

She'd called Heather the night before and told her that she had to get up in front of the entire homeroom and sing the national anthem. Even though Heather had said that would be no problem, Jessica was sure she'd back out at the last minute. After all, she'd clearly make a total fool of herself.

"Hey, Jessica, this is the first time I've seen you here so early," Annie said, sitting down next to Jessica.

"I didn't want to miss the special event," Jessica said excitedly.

"What special event?" Maria asked. "Are we getting a half day for some reason? Are they going to announce it in homeroom?"

"That would be awesome," Lila said. "There's nothing I'd rather do than close my eyes and lie on the beach all afternoon."

"You can hold on to your beach towel, because

we're not getting a half day," Jessica said.

"So what's the big event?" Maria asked. "Don't tell me you're excited to hear the roll call."

"It's a surprise," Jessica said secretively.

"Give us a hint," Lila said.

"OK, Heather's about to do her last cheerleading test," Jessica said. "And you're about to see her fail it before your very eyes."

"Excuse me, everyone! Can I have your attention?" Heather was standing at the front of the classroom. "This morning I'd like to start off homeroom with something a little special."

She sure looks calm and collected for someone who's about to make a total fool of herself, Jessica thought.

Heather opened her mouth, and out came the sounds of a professional singer. All of the students sat perfectly quiet and still as Heather filled the room with her beautiful voice. She did a funky version of the national anthem, and some students were even clapping their hands and snapping their fingers.

How is this possible? Jessica thought. She was furious. Jessica's tests kept backfiring and making Heather an even bigger star.

When Heather finished her song, the classroom went wild. People were jumping up from their seats to congratulate Heather on her performance.

"You sound like a professional singer," Amy gushed.

"You could really go far with your talent," Winston said.

"Well, I've actually had a few offers from different record companies to record a CD," Heather said. "My manager wanted me to pursue a career in music, but my parents want me to finish high school first."

"What exactly were you testing, Jessica?" Maria asked. "We never had a musical tryout as far as I can remember."

"I was trying to see, umm . . . I was trying to see if Heather had the ability to perform in public," Jessica said. "After all, that's what we do as cheerleaders."

"Could you sing another song?" Annie pleaded. "This is the best homeroom we've had all year."

"Sure," Heather said. "I'll sing one I wrote. I even brought my guitar along."

Jessica slid down in her seat in total misery as Heather started to sing a slow, bluesy song. Not only was Heather a great singer, but she was a fantastic guitar player as well. Jessica just couldn't believe that she was responsible for getting more attention for Heather. She had been so sure that Heather would fail her final test. *It's just not fair,*

Jessica thought. *Not only will Heather make it on the squad, she'll be more popular than ever because of me!*

"Well, Heather passed all of your tests, Jessica," Robin said at the beginning of cheerleading practice on Thursday afternoon. "I guess she might as well start practicing with us. I'll go call her over here."

"We haven't taken a vote yet," Jessica said.

"The last time we took a vote, everyone except you was in favor of her joining the team," Robin pointed out. "I'm sure nobody's changed their mind since Monday."

"And those tests you put her through were pretty rigorous," Jean said.

"Yeah, I'm glad I didn't have to do any of those things when I was trying to be a cheerleader," Amy agreed.

"They were just standard tests of confidence, depth, and performance," Jessica explained.

"Well, she passed them, so that's the end of the discussion," Robin snapped uncharacteristically. Clearly she was losing patience with her cocaptain. "Let's get on with it."

Jessica looked up at the bleachers where Heather was waiting. *That girl has some nerve,* Jessica thought.

"A lot can happen in a couple of days," Jessica

said, desperately trying to keep the inevitable from happening. "People might have gotten to know Heather a little bit better. Maybe they see her for what she really is."

"What's that supposed to mean?" Robin asked. "Are you saying there's something we should know about Heather?"

"As a matter of fact, I am saying that," Jessica said. "From what I've seen, she's a fake. She pretends to be really sweet, but the truth is she's not a nice person at all."

"I have to disagree with you," Annie said. "I've spent a lot of time with her since she started school here—a lot more than you have—and I think she's really great. She's nice and funny and totally cool. Just perfect for our squad."

"I agree," Amy said. "Yesterday Heather told me that she started a tutoring program at her old school. She got students to go to the poor areas around her community and help kids with their homework."

"She really sounds like a great role model," Annie said. "I think she could be a positive force for all of us."

"If she joins the sqaud, our standards will really drop," Jessica said forebodingly. "We just haven't known her long enough to see if she's really cheerleading material. People can appear one way on the outside, but the more you get to know them, you see that they were just putting on an act."

"I just don't understand why you have such a thing about Heather," Robin said. "I think you're really being weird about this. What has she done to you that's made you dislike her so much?"

Jessica couldn't really put it into words, and she didn't like Robin calling her weird. In fact, she thought Robin was being unusually testy.

"I was wondering the same thing," Amy said. "Nobody else except you seems to have a problem with her."

Jessica was being put on the spot. She couldn't explain that there was a certain way Heather smiled at her that made her cringe or a smugness about her that rubbed Jessica the wrong way. It was just something she felt so deeply, but it was frustrating not to be able to articulate it. It was more than the fact that Heather kept taking attention away from Jessica.

"It's hard to say exactly what it is," Jessica said. "It's just an attitude that she has that I know would be wrong for our squad. You just have to trust me on this. I'm a good judge of character."

"But she passed all the tests you came up with to test her character," Sandy Bacon said. "They were pretty tough, too. I don't think any of us would have come to school dressed the way she was yesterday. Most of us are too vain."

"It turned out to be a big success for her," Jessica said. "Everyone told her how in style she was."

"But she didn't know it would work out that way for her, and she wore those hideous-looking overalls anyway," Jeannie said.

Jessica felt as if she were being pushed into a corner. *No matter what I say, they're still determined to have her on this squad,* Jessica thought. "I really feel strongly about this, and I think if somebody has such a passionate feeling about something, everyone else has to go along with it."

"That's ridiculous," Robin protested. "That's like saying that if you want something and we don't, we all have to do what you say. If you said we should all jump off the roof of the gymnasium, would we have to do that too?"

"I'm not saying that at all," Jessica said. All of Jessica's points seemed to be getting twisted around, and she wasn't any closer to making her case than when she started.

"Don't forget how opposed you were to Annie joining the squad," Robin said. "Now she's one of the best cheerleaders we have."

Jessica looked at Annie and felt a guilty pang. When Annie first tried to be a cheerleader, Jessica had fought it tooth and nail. She told everyone that Annie was the wrong kind of girl for their squad because she had a reputation for being fast with the guys. Jessica had done everything in her power to keep Annie off the squad, and Annie had ended up trying to kill herself. She had swallowed a bottle of pills and was rushed to the hospital just in time to save her life. *It's really unfair of Robin to bring that up,* Jessica thought. *She knows how bad I feel about what I did. This is different. Heather really is a mean person. Why am I the only person who seems to realize that?*

"This is a totally different situation, and you know it," Jessica protested. She was starting to feel as if everyone was ganging up on her.

"Why don't you just admit that you're jealous of Heather?" Amy blurted out as she stretched over and touched her toes. "It's not a federal offense to be jealous. It happens to everyone. I just think in this case you should put your jealousy aside for the moment and think about what's best for the team."

"First of all, I'm not jealous of Heather, and second of all, I *am* thinking about what's best for the team," Jessica cried. "I can guarantee that voting for Heather to be on our squad will be the biggest mistake you'll ever make."

"Speaking of voting," Robin started, "that's exactly what we're going to do. We've wasted enough time on this discussion as it is. All those in favor of letting Heather on the squad, raise their right hand."

Jessica closed her eyes. She knew that her arguments for keeping Heather off the squad hadn't worked the way she'd hoped they would. She couldn't bear to see everyone raising her hand again.

All the other cheerleaders started clapping and cheering as Jessica opened her eyes. Heather stood up on the bleachers as if she were a movie star and walked slowly down to the field.

"Way to go, Heather!" Robin shouted.

"Congratulations!" Amy added.

"Welcome to the team," Annie said.

"Let's start practice," Jessica commanded, refusing to look Heather in the eye. "We're going to start out with the 'Be Aggressive' cheer." Jessica stood facing the girls, who were in a line. She spread her legs, extended her arms to the side, and started the cheer. "Be aggressive! Be aggressive! B-E-A-G-G-R-E-S-S-I-V-E—"

"Excuse me," Heather yelled, jumping in front of Jessica. "If you don't mind, I have a suggestion that might really make this old, tired cheer a little more hip."

"As a matter of fact, Heather," Jessica said

evenly, trying with all her might not to lose her temper, "I *do* mind! Maybe when I'm finished—"

"Jessica, as the cocaptain," Robin said, stepping out of the line toward Jessica and Heather, "I *would* like to see a new version of this cheer. Even you have to admit that this one is incredibly boring."

"You never said anything about its being boring in the past," Jessica pointed out. *How could she embarrass me like this in front of Heather?* Jessica wondered as she felt her whole body shaking with anger.

"It never occurred to me that there might be a more interesting way of doing it," Robin said.

Jessica watched in horror as Heather proceeded to do the same cheer over again but with a funky rap beat instead. The girls went nuts, and Jessica wanted to punch Heather in the stomach.

"It's like a whole new cheer," Robin enthused. "That was about a hundred times more exciting than the way we do it."

"Do you think you could show us how to do that?" Amy asked.

"Sure, no problem," Heather said. "Just imagine that you're dancing and singing instead of cheering."

"But we're supposed to be cheering," Jessica

63

said, putting her hands on her hips. "That's why we're called *cheer*leaders."

"Jessica, it wouldn't hurt to change our cheer just a little bit," Robin said. "And besides, look at all the girls. They obviously wouldn't mind learning Heather's version."

Jessica knew Robin was right. She looked at the faces of the girls, beaming with admiration for Heather. Jessica reluctantly and angrily stepped to the side and allowed Heather to teach them the cheer *her* way. *I can't stand that girl, and if I have anything to do about it—she won't be on this squad for long!* she vowed to herself.

Chapter 5

Elizabeth felt a chill and pulled her jean jacket around her tightly. She watched the foam crash against the sand and felt the cool water sneak up between her uncovered toes. She'd driven to the beach after school on Thursday to try to clear her head. When she looked out at the enormity of the ocean, her problems always felt smaller and less overwhelming.

She was trying desperately to keep everything in perspective. *I'm sure about my feelings for Todd, and I know I want to be with him,* she told herself as she threw a shell into the water and watched it splash. *I would be miserable if anything caused us to break up.* But as she kept walking, Ken's face continued to creep into her thoughts as it had for the last week.

All day she kept going over her talk with Mr. Collins. How was she supposed to resolve her feelings for Ken if she didn't spend any time with him? She wished that her older brother, Steven, were home from college. He'd be a good person to talk to because he knew her so well and he was good at giving advice.

Elizabeth knew that spending time with Ken now that Jessica was seeing him would be impossible. She kept going back and forth about whether or not to tell Jessica what had happened between her and Ken. *Maybe she will stop seeing him until I figure out my true feelings for him,* Elizabeth thought hopefully. The more she thought about that, though, the more she knew it was absurd. *Knowing my sister, that would probably make her even more determined to see Ken.*

Elizabeth broke into a run along the water's edge. She wanted to run away from everything. Away from the guilt and the jealousy. She felt the sea air burning against her cheeks, and she felt freer and lighter than she had in days.

She saw a figure of someone sitting on the beach, but she couldn't tell who it was from a distance. As she got closer, she realized it was Robin Wilson. *She must have just come from cheerleading practice,* Elizabeth thought as she got closer.

Thinking of cheerleading reminded her of Jessica, and all her problems came flooding back to her.

"What brings you out here?" Elizabeth asked, plopping down on the sand next to Robin. "You look a little glum."

"I'm more than a little glum," Robin said sadly. "I tried to act like everything was normal at practice. As soon as it was over, I jumped in my car and headed for the beach. I can think better here for some reason."

"So can I," Elizabeth said. "It always helps me put things in perspective." Both girls stared out at the horizon over the water. They had never been particularly close friends, but Elizabeth always liked Robin a lot, and in some ways she was happy to be sitting with someone who didn't know her so well. "I can't imagine not living near the ocean. I need it for my sanity."

"That's exactly what I was just thinking," Robin said. "I'm really going to miss this beach—not to mention my friends, the cheering squad, Sweet Valley High, and everything else."

"What are you talking about?" Elizabeth asked, turning to face Robin. "Are you going away somewhere?"

"Yes," Robin said, sighing heavily. "My dad just got a job transfer to Denver, Colorado, and we have to move as soon as possible. I haven't told anyone else yet. I guess I thought if I told anyone, it would make it real."

"You poor thing," Elizabeth said, but really she couldn't help thinking that she would love to be moving away herself. Then she wouldn't have to decide what to do about Ken and Todd and Jessica.

Robin wiped away a tear. "I love it here. I can't stand the idea of having to make all new friends at a different school."

"Maybe if you look at it as an exciting new adventure . . ." Elizabeth said, trying to comfort her. "It's great to have new experiences in life. If you want to know the truth, I'm actually a little envious of you. What I'd give to just move away . . ."

Robin looked at her, surprised. "You? But you always seem so happy. Is something bothering you?"

"Let's just say I have a lot on my mind these days," Elizabeth said, and anxious to change the subject, she stood up and brushed the sand off her sweater and blue jeans. "Come on, I want you to tell me all about Denver on our walk back to the parking lot."

"Can you turn down the CD player? I'm having a hard time concentrating on my English essay," Elizabeth said. She and Jessica were sprawled out in the family room on Thursday night, doing their homework.

"Elizabeth, I'm a little worried about you. It seems like you've been burying your nose in your work a little more than usual lately," Jessica said. "There's more to life than homework, you know."

It was true. Elizabeth had been spending more time on her studies lately—it was the only thing that helped keep her mind off Ken. She was immersing herself in her schoolwork, hoping the whole situation would just go away. But of course it hadn't, and in the meantime she couldn't remember the last time she had just let loose and enjoyed herself. "This happens to be an interesting essay, actually," Elizabeth said for Jessica's benefit. "It's about Zelda Fitzgerald."

"Zelda! Who would ever name their daughter Zelda?" Jessica asked as she walked back from turning down the music.

"She was the wife of the writer F. Scott Fitzgerald," Elizabeth explained patiently. "She was a writer herself, and she lived a really exciting but tragic life."

"Well, I'm living a tragic life right now thanks to the arrival in Sweet Valley of Heather Mallone," Jessica groaned as she flopped down onto the couch. "She's making my life absolutely miserable."

"What has she done to you?" Elizabeth asked, eager to hear about anything that didn't have to do with Jessica's growing romance with Ken.

"Everyone except me voted for her to be on the squad this afternoon," Jessica said.

"What's so bad about that? I've heard she's a really good cheerleader."

"I don't care how good a cheerleader she is," Jessica said. "The point is that she's a horrible, awful person, and I know she's going to be the worst thing that ever happened to our squad. Nobody except me seems to see her truly evil personality."

"Why don't you try looking at the positive side?" Elizabeth suggested.

"And what positive side could there possibly be?" Jessica asked skeptically.

"She obviously has a lot of cheerleading experience," Elizabeth started. "You could probably learn a lot from her. Maybe she'll even improve the squad. After all, her old squad won their state championship, right? Even I know enough about cheerleading to realize that that means she must be a pretty good cheerleader."

"First of all, you really *don't* know anything about cheerleading, although I do appreciate your trying to help. Second of all, if I hear one more time that her squad won state, I'm going to scream."

"I'm just saying she could be a positive influence," Elizabeth said gently.

"As long as I'm one of the captains, she will have no influence on my squad whatsoever," Jessica said.

"If you go into practice every day thinking that you have to fight her, it will be counterproductive for everyone," Elizabeth warned. "I have a great idea—and before you completely reject it—just consider it for a minute. What if you make Heather a cocaptain? That way you'll be working together for the same purpose instead of in conflict with each other."

Jessica laughed. "You're really weird, Liz. I already *have* a cocaptain, as you very well know."

"But Robin's moving to Denver," Elizabeth blurted out, then quickly covered her mouth when she realized what she'd said.

"What are you talking about?" Jessica was sitting straight up on the couch. "You hardly ever even see Robin. How would you know something like that?"

"I'm really sorry I blurted it out like that," Elizabeth said. "I ran into her this afternoon after your practice, and she told me her dad got a new job. It sounds like they're leaving pretty soon."

"Great, now my horrible day is even worse," Jessica said. "Not only am I losing one of my good

71

friends, I'm losing the cocaptain of the squad. Now that I think of it, Robin wasn't really acting like herself today at practice. And she was so adamant about Heather's being on the squad. I guess that's because she was thinking there'd be a new slot left to fill when she leaves."

"So maybe you *will* consider letting Heather be your cocaptain," Elizabeth said.

"I can promise you that Heather Mallone will be my cocaptain just as soon as it snows in Sweet Valley in August," Jessica said. Both girls laughed at her joke.

"My life really is a tragedy like that woman you're writing about," Jessica continued. "But at least I have one thing to be happy about."

"What's that?" Elizabeth asked.

"My date tomorrow night with Ken," Jessica said dreamily. "I wish I could just go to sleep and wake up tomorrow night. I can't wait!"

And once again Elizabeth felt as if someone had knocked the breath out of her.

"I just can't believe you're leaving," Amy said. "I'm going to miss you so much."

"It's too sad to even think about," Annie said. "Let's just not think about it."

It was Friday at lunch, and Robin had just announced she was moving. Everyone at the table was teary-eyed. Jessica hated that Heather was sitting at their table at such a sad and personal time. After all, Heather was really still a stranger.

"I could see if my parents would let you come and live with us," Lila said excitedly. "There's obviously more than enough room, and it would be a total blast."

"You're really nice to offer that, but I seriously doubt my parents would go for it," Robin said, forcing a weak smile.

"Do you think you'll come back and visit us?" Helen asked.

"My parents promised me that they'd let me come back and visit all the time," Robin said. "Denver's not so far from Sweet Valley. Maybe you guys could come and visit me for a ski trip sometime."

"That would be awesome," Jeannie said.

"I'm really going to miss you guys," Robin said. "And I'm especially going to miss being on the cheerleading squad. I feel like I'm letting you all down."

"I don't want you to worry about that," Jessica said. "I'm fully prepared to be the only captain when you leave. It won't be the same without you, but I'm going to keep the squad together."

"Don't you think that will be hard to just have

one captain?" Heather asked. "I mean, a good squad really needs two captains."

"Hi, Heather!" said Charles Stewart, one of the nerdiest guys on the chess team, as he passed by the table.

"Oh, hey, Chuck!" Heather waved and flashed one of her toothy smiles.

"Excuse me," Jessica said, annoyed by the reminder that all her tests for Heather had backfired, making her more popular than ever. "I believe we were in the middle of a conversation about cheerleading."

"Oh, right. I was saying that it's next to impossible to have one captain for a squad," Heather said.

"And I was about to say that I'm perfectly capable of leading the squad by myself," Jessica said defensively. Even though she was definitely going to miss Robin, part of Jessica was secretly starting to get excited by the idea of being the only captain.

"Being the only captain of a squad is an enormous responsibility, especially if you're interested in taking your squad on to competitions," Heather said.

"I have an idea!" Amy was beaming with excitement. "Since Heather has so much experience, why don't we make her the new cocaptain!"

Jessica was fuming. *Over my dead body!* she wanted to shout. But before she could say anything, Helen had started talking.

"All those in favor of Heather being the new cocaptain, raise their right hand," Helen said.

Everyone on the squad raised her right hand except Jessica, who was practically in shock. She couldn't believe that she was really going to be leading the squad with Heather. The thought was too incredible to take in.

"It looks like we have a new cocaptain," Annie said. "I hope we'll measure up to your standards."

"Oh, I'm sure you will," Heather said. "I am absolutely thrilled by the honor."

"I feel better now that I know the squad will be left in the capable hands of Jessica and Heather," Robin said.

"I'm really looking forward to working with you, Jessica," Heather said in that fake voice of hers.

Jessica was so upset she couldn't even speak. She looked across the table at Heather, who was beaming at Jessica with a sickening smile. Now the one thing that Jessica loved more than anything—cheerleading—was ruined because of Heather Mallone.

"Is *that* what you're wearing on your date?" Elizabeth asked Jessica later that night as she opened the door of the bathroom that connected their two bedrooms. "That looks like a nightie."

Elizabeth was referring to the white sundress Jessica was wearing that came way above her knee and was cut low in front. It was very sexy—too sexy, in Elizabeth's opinion—and it showed off Jessica's perfectly tan, fit body. The thought of Ken seeing her sister in that dress was enough to make Elizabeth want to lock Jessica in the house.

"You've seen me wear this dress about a zillion times before, and you've never said anything about it," Jessica said as she flipped her head over to brush the underside of her hair.

"I just don't think it's appropriate for tonight," Elizabeth said, trying to sound sincere.

"I can't think of a more appropriate time to wear it than tonight," Jessica said. "I'm going on my first real date with a gorgeous guy who happens to be the quarterback of the football team and who I'm absolutely crazy about. If this isn't the right occasion to wear this dress, then I don't know what is."

But you can't wear that dress tonight, because I might still be interested in Ken, Elizabeth wanted to say. "Well, maybe you should wear a jacket over it."

Elizabeth left the bathroom, then came right

76

back carrying her pink oversize knit sweater. "Here, this would look great over it. It could get chilly tonight."

"Liz, are you a total moron? I'm going on a date, not on a picnic with a kindergarten class."

"Well, you don't have to wear this sweater, but you should wear something over that dress," Elizabeth said. "You don't want to look too—"

"Too what?" Jessica asked, putting on bright-red lipstick. "Too sexy? Sexy is *exactly* what I want to look like."

"But Ken's not that kind of guy," Elizabeth said.

"Not what kind of guy?" Jessica laughed. "Not the kind of guy who likes pretty girls?"

"I know he's Todd's best friend and everything, but he's a pretty boring guy," Elizabeth lied. "He'll probably think a sexy dress is a total turnoff. Ken's a real snore, Jessica. I only tolerate him because of Todd."

"If Ken's a snore, then Todd's a coma," Jessica teased.

"No, really," Elizabeth continued, ignoring her sister's slight to Todd. "Ken's actually very serious, and I'd imagine that he'd prefer a girl who was a little more bookish—less flashy."

"You're way off base, Liz. And no offense, but I do believe I'm the expert when it comes to guys."

"I just think you need to go slowly," Elizabeth said, grasping at straws.

"The greatest thing about Ken is that I really feel like he's a friend of mine," Jessica said, making a pouting face in the mirror to see if her makeup looked OK. "I mean, I feel like I can talk to him about anything. I can't wait to tell him about what happened today with the cheerleading squad. He's so supportive and understanding. I know he'll totally be on my side when I tell him how horrible that Heather is."

He is a good person to talk to, Elizabeth thought as she remembered all the hours she and Ken had stayed up talking about life and literature and love and everything else under the sun.

"So how do I look?" Jessica asked as she turned to face her sister.

"Beautiful," Elizabeth said morosely. "Just beautiful."

Elizabeth's heart sank as she walked out of the bathroom, swallowing back the tears.

Chapter 6

"I'll get it," Elizabeth yelled as she bounded down the stairs to open the door for Todd. They were going to the movies, and she was anxious to get out of the house and get her mind off Jessica's date.

When she opened the door, her heart stopped. Instead of looking at Todd, she was looking at Ken. For some reason she had thought Jessica was meeting Ken somewhere else. It never occurred to her that he would come to their house. He looked as stunned to see Elizabeth as she was to see him.

"Hi, Elizabeth," Ken practically whispered as he looked down at his feet.

Elizabeth noticed that he was holding his hands behind his back. *He brought flowers*, she realized sadly. *He brought flowers for my sister and not for me.*

"Hi, Ken," Elizabeth said. She felt as if she were talking with marbles in her mouth. Until recently they'd been able to talk to each other normally, but tonight she could barely say two words to him.

They just stood there silently, both afraid to be the first one to speak. Ken continued to avoid eye contact with Elizabeth. *Look at me,* Elizabeth wanted to say. *Talk to me about what happened between us. Tell me what your feelings are toward me. Tell me that you're not really interested in Jessica.*

"Hi, Ken!" Jessica said excitedly as she practically leaped down the stairs. She threw her arms around Ken's neck and gave him a kiss on the cheek. "Boy, am I glad to see *you*. You're not going to believe what happened to me today."

Elizabeth kept standing there and watched Ken as his face turned bright red. *He's embarrassed by this situation because he remembers what happened between us,* Elizabeth thought. That made her feel better somehow. At least he remembered their secret past.

"We should get going," Ken said timidly.

"Are those flowers for me?" Jessica asked as she grabbed the flowers from behind Ken's back. "That was so sweet of you."

Jessica handed the flowers to Elizabeth. "Liz,

80

we're in a hurry. Could you be a doll and put these flowers in water for me?"

Before Elizabeth could answer, Ken and Jessica were in Ken's car, and she was standing there holding a beautiful bouquet of roses that wasn't meant for her. Elizabeth watched as they drove away, leaving her alone in her misery.

"You look great tonight," Todd said to Elizabeth as he nuzzled up to her neck. They were sitting in the Sweet Valley movie theater before the previews had started. "And you smell wonderful, as usual."

He is so sweet, Elizabeth thought. She had thrown on a denim shirt and blue jeans and pulled the front part of her hair back in a barrette, and here he was acting as if she were dressed for the prom. Elizabeth felt a familiar twinge of guilt. *He's so good to me and he loves me so much. How can I even think about another guy?*

As hard as she tried to concentrate on Todd and to stop thinking about Jessica and Ken, she couldn't help wondering where they were right at that moment and what they were doing. She kept having an image of Jessica in that skimpy white dress, and she wondered if Ken thought she looked sexy. *Of course he does,* Elizabeth thought. *But it doesn't matter anyway, because you're sitting right here with your wonderful boyfriend who adores you,* she told herself.

"All week I look forward to Friday night so I can be with you without worrying about getting up early for school the next day," Todd said. "You're what gets me through the week."

Elizabeth gave Todd a big kiss on the lips.

"What was that for?" Todd asked, obviously pleased by Elizabeth's show of affection.

"Because I love you," Elizabeth said. She leaned her head on his shoulder, and for one moment her jealous thoughts were almost gone.

Todd pointed toward the front of the theater. "Look who's here."

Elizabeth looked in the direction where Todd was pointing. She couldn't believe it. Ken and Jessica were sitting down just five rows in front of them.

"Ken was really excited about their date," Todd said. "That's all he was talking about this afternoon. I even went to the florist with him. He spent about twenty minutes choosing the right flowers to bring your sister."

"The movie's about to start," Elizabeth said. She couldn't say anything else. She couldn't even pretend to be excited about Jessica and Ken and their stupid date.

The lights went down and the movie started.

Elizabeth wasn't watching the movie. She couldn't take her eyes off her sister and Ken. She watched as Ken put his arm around the back of Jessica's chair. *Stop looking at them,* she told herself. She just couldn't stop torturing herself. Jessica turned toward Ken in that flirtatious smile Elizabeth knew too well, and whispered something to him. Ken leaned down and gave Jessica a little kiss on the lips.

Elizabeth felt as if a knife were going through her heart. She kept remembering times that she and Ken had gone to movies together. They had sat in the back together and whispered like that to each other, and he had kissed her sweetly when nobody was watching. *How can he do the same things with her?* Even though Elizabeth knew she had no right to be mad at Ken—she was with Todd, after all—she was furious. She felt betrayed.

Does he like Jessica more than he liked me? Does he like kissing her more? Does he think she's sexier than me? Does he like talking to her better? Elizabeth kept thinking the same thoughts over and over again, and throughout the movie her gaze never left the happy couple sitting just five rows in front of her.

"I loved that movie," Jessica enthused. She was sitting at a booth at Casey's Ice Cream Parlor with

Ken, Todd, and Elizabeth. They'd all run into each other in front of the movie theater, and Todd had suggested that they get some ice cream together. So far it had been a great evening. She and Ken had whispered and giggled and held hands during the entire movie.

"I thought that the acting was great," Todd said. "But the plot didn't really hold up. I mean, how realistic is it that that woman would have married the same man in a second life?"

"I think the point is that it's a *movie*," Jessica teased. "It's not real life. Now I see why you and Elizabeth get along so well—you're both as serious and practical as the other one."

"How did you like it, Ken?" Todd asked.

"Oh, I liked it a lot," Ken said. "And I really liked all the scenes that took place in the first life of the characters."

"Me too," Jessica said, moving closer to Ken in the booth. She thought Ken seemed a little distracted, but she decided it was probably just because he was still a little nervous. They *were* on their first date, after all. "Those costumes they were wearing in that ball scene were gorgeous."

"What about you, Elizabeth? What was your favorite scene?" Todd asked.

Elizabeth looked up from her sundae as if she'd been in another galaxy. She'd been acting totally spaced out ever since they'd sat down in the booth. "I'm not sure."

"What planet are you on?" Jessica asked her sister. "You seem really out of it."

"I'm just thinking about the movie," Elizabeth said weakly. "I liked it a lot, but I can't decide which scene was my favorite."

"Hey, kids!" a female voice said from behind Jessica.

Jessica looked up from her banana split and saw Heather looking down at her. She was standing by their booth, surrounded by about four or five guys who were practically drooling all over her.

"How are you, Jessica?" Heather asked in her supersweet voice. "That's a serious banana split you're eating. I can't imagine what the fat count for that would be."

Jessica remembered how rude Heather had been that first day about the fettuccine she was eating. It had been all Jessica could do not to pick up her plate and throw it into Heather's face, but tonight she was having such a good time with Ken that not even Heather could bother her.

"Would you like a bite? It's delicious," Jessica said, delicately taking a bite of whipped cream, vanilla ice cream, and butterscotch sauce.

"No, thanks, but I would like a bite of Ken's

hot-fudge sundae," Heather said, smiling flirtatiously at Ken.

Jessica looked at Ken, who was smiling back at Heather. She watched in horror as Heather leaned over their table and opened her mouth while Ken fed her a bite of his sundae.

"Thanks, that was yummy," Heather said, licking her lips. "It's amazing that you're able to stay in such great shape and eat sweets like that, Ken."

"I'll just have to jog an extra mile or two tomorrow," Ken said.

"Are you a jogger?" Heather asked.

"Yeah, I jog every day," Ken said.

"So do I," Heather said, as if it were the most interesting thing in the world. "I've been looking for someone to jog with. Maybe we could start jogging together. Why don't you give me a call?"

"Sure thing," Ken said.

Jessica's blood was boiling. *The nerve of that awful girl flirting with my date right in front of me,* Jessica thought as she watched Heather slink away. *She's got another thing coming if she thinks she can make a move on my guy!*

Jessica looked at Elizabeth, who looked as upset about Heather's little flirtation as she was. *That's a loyal sister,* Jessica thought lovingly. *She's protective of me and my date. I'm lucky to have her on my side.*

"I wouldn't worry about Heather," Ken said. He and Jessica were sitting in his car in front of the Wakefields' house after they'd left Casey's. Jessica had just finished telling him about how Heather was going to be the new cocaptain. "You're a fantastic cheerleading captain, and there's no way she could possibly compete with you."

"Do you really think so?"

"Absolutely," Ken said, looking deeply into Jessica's eyes.

"She *is* really pretty," Jessica said, trying to see what Ken's reaction would be. She was still a little jealous about the way Heather had been flirting with him at the Dairi Burger.

"*You're* the one who's really pretty, and in fact, you're looking exceptionally beautiful tonight," Ken said as he took a strand of Jessica's hair in his fingers and twirled it around. "You really take my breath away."

"So you don't think you'll be calling her like she asked you to?" Jessica asked, trying to sound as if it were an innocent question.

"No way," Ken said. "Why would I ever want to call her? I'd rather call you *any*day."

"I had a great time with you tonight," Jessica said.

"So did I."

"I'm glad to hear that. I was worried there for a minute. You were almost as quiet as my sister was at Casey's."

"I guess I just wanted to be alone with you," Ken said.

Jessica was dying for him to kiss her. At Casey's she couldn't wait to get away from her sister and Todd so she could be alone with Ken. *I can tell he really likes me, and I know he would never hurt me the way Jeremy did,* she thought as he leaned toward her. *He's too nice a guy to do that. Elizabeth was wrong to warn me about going slowly with my feelings.*

"I feel really comfortable with you, Ken," Jessica said. "And I've been wanting to tell you how much your friendship meant to me when I was going through that hard time recently."

"I hope you think of me as more than just a friend," Ken said.

"I think that's pretty obvious," Jessica said. She put her face close to his and closed her eyes. Ken kissed her so tenderly that Jessica felt as if she never wanted the kiss to end.

"Excuse me, but I believe this dress has J-E-S-S-I-C-A written all over it," Jessica said as she walked out of the fitting room at Bibi's. "This is exactly what I want to wear to Amy's going-away party for Robin tonight."

"You're not seriously thinking of buying a new dress just for one party, are you?" Elizabeth asked. "That's pretty indulgent, if you ask me."

It was Saturday afternoon, and the twins were spending the day at the mall. Elizabeth had been in a bad mood all day. Last night had been a nightmare. It was pure torture sitting with Ken and Jessica on their date. She could tell that Ken was as uncomfortable as she was. He wouldn't look at her the entire time they were sitting in the booth at Casey's. And it was torture to watch her sister flirting with Ken right in front of her.

She didn't want to spend the day with her sister, but Jessica had insisted she go to the mall with her. Every time Jessica would start talking about Ken, Elizabeth tried to change the subject.

"First of all, it's not like I'm only going to wear it tonight and never again," Jessica said as she posed in front of the mirror to see what it looked like from all different angles. "And besides, I'm really buying it to look good for Ken tonight."

"It makes you look fat," Elizabeth blurted out.

Jessica looked mortified. "Are you saying I've gained weight?" She scrutinized herself in the mirror. "I have been eating a lot of banana splits at the Dairi Burger and Casey's recently."

"No, I just think that dress isn't very flattering on you," Elizabeth said. The truth was that the dress looked fabulous on Jessica—a little too fabulous. She didn't want Jessica to look so good for Ken. It was totally out of character for Elizabeth to lie to her sister like that, but she couldn't help it.

"That dress fits you like a glove," the salesgirl said as she passed Jessica.

"Really?" Jessica asked excitedly. "My sister thinks it makes me look fat. What do you think?"

"I think your sister needs glasses," the salesgirl said. "You're as skinny as a rail."

"That settles it," Jessica said. "I'm going to take it."

"I didn't realize Ken was taking you to the party," Elizabeth said as she followed Jessica into the changing room. "Did he actually call and invite you to go together?" Elizabeth was pretty sure he hadn't called, but she couldn't resist placing a little doubt in Jessica's mind.

"No, he didn't," Jessica said. "But I know he'll be at the party, and I'm sure we'll be there as a couple."

"Hmmm," Elizabeth said, trying to sound doubtful.

"What?" Jessica asked, obviously worried.

"It's nothing," Elizabeth said, making a face that implied the exact opposite.

"Come on, Liz," Jessica pleaded. "Tell me what's wrong."

"I just think it's odd that Ken wouldn't have invited you as his date to the party," Elizabeth said. "I mean, the party is for one of your best friends, and if you're really starting to be a couple, I don't know why he wouldn't want to take you out in public."

Jessica scrunched up her face as if she were concentrating on a really difficult math problem. "I never thought of that. I know he really likes me a lot, though, so I don't think I have anything to worry about."

"You're probably right," Elizabeth said. "But I'd be careful if I were you. Heather Mallone sure looks like she's trying to get her claws in him."

"Why do you say that?"

"Well, she was falling all over him at Casey's last night," Elizabeth said, hating herself for making her sister worry. "She seems like someone who usually gets what she wants. She certainly succeeded in becoming your cocaptain."

"I'm not afraid of her. I can handle Heather," Jessica declared as she walked out of the dressing room with the dress in hand. "Ken even said to me that he didn't think she was pretty."

"I guess he *would* tell you that," Elizabeth said. "I mean, he wouldn't come right out and tell you if he liked her, I guess. Did you ever think he might just have said that because he knew that's what you'd want to hear?"

"I suppose so," Jessica said, handing the dress to the salesgirl at the counter. "Liz, why are you trying to make me paranoid about Ken?"

"I just don't want you to get hurt," Elizabeth said.

"I appreciate your concern, but I can take care of myself," Jessica said. "Don't worry about me. I'll be fine."

That's what I'm worried about, Elizabeth thought. *Things with Ken might be a little too good.*

Chapter 7

"Attention, everybody! I want to make a speech! It is my party, after all," Robin shouted above the noise. It was Saturday night, and Amy was throwing a good-bye party for Robin in her backyard. Some people were standing on the patio around the pool drinking exotic nonalcoholic drinks, and others were dancing on the lawn.

Jessica was really sad about Robin leaving, but she was just a little bit thrilled to have an occasion to get dressed up and see Ken again. She'd thought about him all day long, and it was almost too good to be true that she was seeing him two nights in a row. She was enormously pleased with the peach linen minidress she'd bought that day. When she'd tried it on, she'd known it was a "must buy," in spite of Elizabeth's trying to discourage her.

Jessica was so sure about Ken's feelings for her that she didn't even mind that he hadn't come by to pick her up for the party. After all, it was a last-minute party, since Robin had announced she was leaving only the day before. All of the doubts Elizabeth had expressed to her at the mall didn't worry Jessica. She knew her sister was overprotective of her. She'd always been that way. When Jessica had first started seeing Jeremy, Elizabeth had practically physically prevented her from going out with him. Unfortunately, in that case Elizabeth's fears had been justified, but it was an entirely different situation with Ken. She decided not to be annoyed by her sister's warnings. She knew Elizabeth was behaving that way only out of love and concern. Luckily, she knew she had nothing to worry about as far as Ken was concerned.

Jessica turned to look at Robin, who was giving her speech, but she was also trying to strike a sexy pose for Ken, who was standing on the other side of the pool.

"I am going to miss all of you so much," Robin was saying as she obviously tried to fight back the tears. "I can't imagine what my life will be like without all of you in it. One thing I'm really going to miss is the pleasure I get from being a cheerleader here. But I'm pleased to officially announce that Heather Mallone will be my replacement as the cocaptain of the cheerleading squad. I know she and Jessica will lead the squad in their continued support of the Gladiators, the best football team in California!"

People cheered and applauded, and a couple of guys shouted, "Babearama!" and "What a dish!"

Jessica had managed to forget about Heather and cheerleading for the time being and resented this ugly reminder.

"Hey, Jessica, how was your date last night?" Lila asked Jessica as she bounded up next to her. "I want a full report."

"Let's just say it was a night I'll never forget," Jessica said, sighing heavily. She was happy to have her thoughts taken away from Heather for the moment. "Ken's the greatest guy in the world. I can't believe I've known him all these years but I'm just now realizing how terrific he is."

"It looks like you're not the only person who thinks so," Lila said. "Check out the action by the refreshment table."

Jessica turned around and, to her horror, saw Heather talking to Ken! They were standing by the table, which was at the edge of the pool, and Heather was laughing loudly and gesticulating wildly.

"That girl is seriously out to ruin my life,"

Jessica fumed. "It's bad enough that she's moving in on my cheerleading domain. Now she has to go after my guy."

"Well, I'm sure that if Ken is as great as you say he is, you'll have nothing to worry about," Lila said. "Although Heather *is* dressed rather seductively. I guess he'd have to be superhuman to resist her charms."

Jessica scrutinized Heather from across the pool. She was wearing high heels, a supertight pink miniskirt, and a white halter top, and her long blond hair was curlier and fuller than ever.

"First of all, Ken has already told me that he's not the least bit interested in Heather," Jessica said. "And I think Heather is wearing about the tackiest outfit I've ever seen."

"But you have to admit she's got an awesome body," Lila said. "I mean, I'd kill for legs like that."

Jessica glared at Lila. "I think Ken is smart enough to see past a good pair of legs," she said, trying to sound calm.

"I kind of like her," Lila said. "Do you really think she's that bad?"

"I knew she was bad news since the first moment I laid eyes on her," Jessica said. "I can't stand that girl."

"So I guess you're really excited about being a cocaptain with her," Lila said sarcastically.

"I *hate* the idea of being a cocaptain with her," Jessica said, feeling her face turn red. "I've put too much work in the squad to let some *interloper* take it away from me."

Heather and Ken were still talking to each other, and it was more than Jessica could take. Her dislike for Heather was stronger than ever, but she had a sudden feeling of power. *I'm not going to let her destroy what I've worked so hard to create*, Jessica thought. *I'm going to show her who's in charge, and I'm going to start right now.*

Jessica walked over to Ken and Heather, ready to do battle. "What a cute little bitty skirt you're wearing," Jessica said, smiling.

"Thanks," Heather said, posing with one hip out by the side of the pool. "I just bought it at the mall today. It was hard to find anything halfway decent there. This was the only thing that wasn't totally hideous."

"I know what you mean," Jessica lied, flashing Heather a bright smile. "Come on, Ken, why don't we dance?"

"Great idea," Ken said.

Jessica slid her arm through Ken's and as she did she "accidentally" bumped into Heather. Heather, teetering on her high heels, tried to regain her balance—she even reached out for Jessica so she wouldn't fall. But Jessica artfully stepped away, leaving Heather to fall into the pool with an unceremonious splash.

"Oh, Heather, I'm so sorry!" Jessica said when Heather surfaced, her long blond curls a sodden mess and mascara dripping down her face. "I'm so clumsy sometimes. And you were wearing your brand-new skirt. Oh, and Heather, a word to the wise: always were waterproof mascara to pool parties."

And with that Jessica walked away, hand in hand with Ken, enormously pleased with herself. *Now she'll know who she's doing business with,* Jessica thought triumphantly.

"Those two really look like they're getting serious," Todd said to Elizabeth as they slow-danced at the party for Robin. "If they stand any closer together, they'll have to be surgically removed."

Elizabeth didn't need to have it pointed out to her that her sister and Ken were extremely cozy on the dance floor. She'd barely taken her eyes from them since they'd started dancing. "Can we not talk about Jessica and Ken?" Elizabeth asked.

"Sure, but I thought you'd be happy about the two of them being together," Todd said. "It's pretty neat that my best friend and your twin sister are a couple. We could have a lot of fun together double-dating and stuff. As you know, I'm not crazy about Jessica, but with you and Ken there, it could be cool."

"I *am* excited about their being together, but I just want to concentrate on you and me," Elizabeth said, putting her head against Todd's chest. The more Todd talked about Ken and Jessica, the guiltier Elizabeth felt. But Elizabeth didn't know which feeling was stronger—her guilt or her jealousy.

Elizabeth looked at her sister, whose face was right up against Ken's. They were speaking to each other in an extremely intimate way, and Elizabeth was dying to know what they were talking about. They were so wrapped up in each other that they barely even moved to the music.

Elizabeth couldn't stand it any longer. She started to move Todd gently in Jessica and Ken's direction. When the two couples were right next to each other, Elizabeth saw that her sister and Ken were about to kiss.

"Why don't we change partners?" Elizabeth suggested suddenly. She ignored the irritated look Jessica shot her way.

"That's a great idea," Todd said. "Hey, Ken, can I cut in?"

Suddenly Elizabeth was standing in front of Ken, and she felt her heart pumping ten times its normal rate.

"How've you been, Liz?" Ken asked awkwardly. He was still avoiding Elizabeth's gaze, just as he'd done the night before when he'd come to pick up Jessica for their date.

"Fine," Elizabeth murmured. Now that she'd arranged to dance with Ken, she was unable even to speak to him.

What's wrong with me? She felt her palms get sweaty as Ken put one hand on her waist and another on her shoulder. They started to sway slowly to the music, when Elizabeth felt as if she was going to be sick. *This is too weird,* she realized. It was almost harder for her to be close to Ken like that in front of everyone, unable to talk about their shared secret, than it was to see him at a distance.

"I'm sorry, Ken, but I have to go." Before Ken had a chance to respond, Elizabeth ran into the house and headed for the bathroom, where she wiped away the tear that had fallen down her cheek.

"I love that dress you're wearing," Ken said to Jessica after most people had left Amy's party. They were sitting close together on the edge of the

100

pool, dangling their feet in the water. Only a few couples, Robin's close friends and their dates, were left, and the only light came from inside the pool. "It's a great color on you."

"Thanks, I've had it forever," Jessica lied. She certainly wasn't going to tell Ken she'd bought it just for him. They'd had only one real date so far, and she didn't want to scare him away.

"This was a great party," Ken said. "I love dancing with you. You're a terrific dancer."

"I do like to dance," Jessica said. "I felt terrible about Heather falling in the pool like that. I guess I was just a little overeager to get to the dance floor."

"She seemed pretty upset," Ken said. "She went home right after that."

"Well," Jessica said, "I just hope she realizes it was an accident and doesn't think I did it on purpose."

"Why would she think that?" Ken asked.

"I don't think she likes me very much," Jessica said in her most innocent voice. "She's a little competitive with me."

"That's understandable," Ken said. "You *are* really popular and pretty. I'm sure a lot of girls are jealous of you."

"You really say the sweetest things," Jessica said.

"I just call it like I see it," Ken said, kissing Jessica on the cheek.

"Speaking of saying things, what did you say to my sister tonight?" Jessica asked.

Jessica noticed that Ken's whole body seemed to tense up, and he moved away from Jessica a few inches. "Nothing," he said abruptly and defensively. "I didn't say anything to her. Why do you ask?"

"I'm not suggesting that you said anything mean to her," Jessica said, confused by his reaction. "It's just that she ran off while she was dancing with you. She looked upset about something. I just thought you might know what she was upset about."

"I have no idea," Ken said. "Maybe you should ask her."

Ken's whole demeanor was suddenly different. He seemed nervous and upset, and Jessica couldn't figure out what she'd said that had got him so agitated.

"Maybe she and Todd were having a fight or something," Jessica said. "Whatever it is, I'm sure it's not very interesting. I love my sister, but she *is* pretty boring."

Ken was staring off in the distance, and he seemed miles away. "I wouldn't know," Ken said quietly.

"She's been kind of weird lately," Jessica said.

102

"How do you mean?" Ken asked.

"She keeps warning me about you," Jessica said.

"Warning you how? What did she say about me?" Ken's attention was focused back on Jessica, and he seemed intensely interested all of a sudden.

Maybe he's just worried that I'm going to stop liking him, Jessica reasoned. *He doesn't want Elizabeth to say anything negative about him that would turn me away from him.*

"She's just protective of me," Jessica said. "She didn't say anything bad about you, don't worry. Elizabeth would warn me about *anyone* I was dating right now. She doesn't want to see me get hurt again like I was by Jeremy."

"Oh, well, she doesn't have anything to worry about," Ken said, putting his arm around Jessica and breathing a sigh of relief. "I should get you home. It's after midnight, and we don't want your sister worrying about you."

Jessica knew she should have Ken take her home, because for some reason she felt unusually tired, and her shoulders had that aching feeling she got whenever she was about to get sick. She knew she ought to get some sleep, because getting sick now was the last thing she needed, but she couldn't bear to leave Ken.

Let her worry, Jessica thought as Ken kissed

her on the lips. Jessica was in heaven. She never wanted their kiss to end.

"I can't believe you're leaving tomorrow morning," Annie said as tears streamed down her face. "This all feels so sudden."

"I know, I feel like my whole life is changing overnight," Robin said between little sobs. "I don't want to say good-bye, though. Let's just all say we'll see each other later—kind of pretend like this isn't happening."

Robin was saying good night to her girlfriends after the party while their dates waited outside in their cars.

"Just think of all the good stuff you have to look forward to," Jessica said.

"Like what?" Robin asked, sniffing.

"Like all the boys to have crushes on, and all the new stores to discover," Jessica said.

"But I'm going to miss my friends like crazy," Robin said.

"You'll make new friends instantly," Amy said.

"They won't be like you guys," Robin said. "They'll never be as much fun."

"We love you, Robin," Annie said as everyone gave Robin a big group hug.

"I love you guys," Robin said, and the tears really started to flow. "Let's always stay in touch."

Jessica was glad Heather wasn't there to spoil

that moment. *Good thing I sent her running home in those wet clothes,* she thought. *Otherwise, I'm sure she'd be here faking her own tears.*

"We'll always be here for you," Jeannie said. "You can come back for big parties and proms. We'll just pretend like you're going on a long vacation."

Jessica wished she *could* pretend. *Then Heather wouldn't be my cocaptain, and my life as I know it wouldn't be ruined!* she thought.

Elizabeth was lying on a lounge chair by the Wakefields' pool on Sunday afternoon while Jessica worked on her cheers nearby. It was a beautiful afternoon, and Elizabeth was determined to stay in a good mood. She'd jumped out of bed that morning telling herself that she just had to forget about Ken. Whatever happened between him and Jessica was beyond her control. Besides, she already had a terrific boyfriend whom she loved.

She'd given herself the opportunity to be close to Ken the night before, and she'd blown it. *Maybe I don't like Ken as much as I thought,* Elizabeth decided as she closed her eyes and enjoyed feeling the sun against her skin.

"I'm coming up with the best cheers I've ever done," Jessica said, startling Elizabeth out of her thoughts. "They're going to blow Heather out of the water. I've decided that I'm not going to let her get me down."

"That's great," Elizabeth said. Because Elizabeth had been feeling guilty about the jealous feelings she'd been having toward her sister, she was glad that things were going better for her in terms of her cheerleading. "That sounds like the Jessica Wakefield we all know and love."

"I'm working on a cheer that has a salsa influence," Jessica said. "Here—watch."

Elizabeth watched as Jessica showed her her new routine. Elizabeth was about as bored by cheerleading as a person could be, but she feigned interest for Jessica's sake. She knew how important cheerleading was to her. Sometimes Elizabeth worried that it was a little *too* important.

"Bravo," Elizabeth said, clapping her hands. "That was great."

"Could you tell that it had a salsa influence?" Jessica asked. "I tried to add a few dance steps and rhythms that I saw in that movie I rented about salsa dancing."

"I definitely see the salsa influence," Elizabeth lied. She couldn't tell the difference between one silly cheer and the next, but she didn't need to tell Jessica that. "I'm glad you're not letting Heather bother you anymore."

"I think one reason I'm not letting Heather get to me is because of Ken," Jessica said.

Please don't talk about Ken, Elizabeth wanted to say to her sister. She'd been trying so hard to put him out of her mind.

"What does Ken have to do with Heather?" Elizabeth asked, not sure that she really wanted to know the answer.

"He's just so incredible," Jessica said, bending down to stretch. "On Friday night we had a long talk about Heather and cheerleading, and he really made me feel confident about my cheerleading abilities. He also made me realize that Heather is really nothing special."

"What did he say exactly?"

"He just said that he didn't think Heather was all that pretty," Jessica said. "In fact, he said she was boring looking."

Elizabeth felt relieved—not because of Jessica's interest in Ken, but because of her own. She had been a little jealous on Friday night when Heather was flirting with him at Casey's. *But I shouldn't feel relieved,* she told herself. *I shouldn't feel anything at all. I just decided I don't care about him anymore.*

"So it sounds like you and Ken are good friends," Elizabeth said, trying to sound cool. "I mean, it sounds like maybe you're *just* friends."

"We *are* friends," Jessica said, getting that annoying, dreamy look in her eye she'd been getting every time she mentioned Ken lately. "But the really wonderful thing is that we're also *more* than just friends. In fact, I think we're getting pretty serious."

"One date is not exactly serious," Elizabeth said. She knew she was bursting Jessica's bubble, but she couldn't help it.

"That was just the beginning. Last night, when we were slow-dancing—and I mean *slow*-dancing—Ken asked me out again for this coming Friday," Jessica said as she leaped into a cartwheel.

"What are you going to do?" Elizabeth knew that she should stop asking questions for her own good, but she couldn't.

"He wouldn't say," Jessica said, coming back up into a standing position. "He just said he wanted to do something extra special. I can't wait. I wish it was tomorrow. I don't know how I'll get through the entire week!"

"Jess, I really think you need to watch out," Elizabeth warned. "I mean, I'm really happy that he asked you out again, but I just think you should be careful."

"Ken is so wonderful," Jessica said. "Of all people he's the last person who would ever hurt anyone. I'm surprised you would doubt that. He *is* Todd's best friend, after all."

"I know that, but sometimes you never really

know about a person," Elizabeth said. "You had no idea that Jeremy was going to turn out to be the kind of jerk that he is. Sometimes appearances are deceiving."

"But it's not like I just met Ken," Jessica said. "I've known him since kindergarten, and so have you, for that matter. I thought you'd be really happy for me."

"I *am* happy for you," Elizabeth lied. "I just think you should take it slowly, that's all. Also, I just don't see how you and Ken could ever work as a couple."

"Why is that?"

"You just seem so different from each other," Elizabeth said. "I mean, you're a lot more fun than he is. He's a pretty serious guy."

"Haven't you ever heard the expression 'Opposites attract'?" Jessica asked. "Besides, look at you and me."

"What about us?"

"Well, we're both totally different and we get along—most of the time," Jessica said.

"Just watch out," Elizabeth said. "It might seem great now, but anything could happen."

"I really wish you'd stop raining on my parade," Jessica said, picking up her pom-poms. "All I want is a little excitement about the fact that I've found a new guy that I really like. Instead all I'm getting is negative warnings."

Jessica walked back into the house, and once again Elizabeth felt terrible about how she'd discouraged Jessica from being with Ken. She was still so confused about her own feelings for him. One minute she thought she was over him, but then, as soon as Jessica started talking about him, she realized that maybe she wasn't. *How am I ever going to know how I really feel about Ken?* she asked herself. *Would I even be thinking about him at all if Jessica weren't seeing him?*

"We gotta fight—fight—with all our might. We gotta dance—dance—and take a chance. We gotta win—win—and do a spin," Jessica wrote on Sunday night after dinner. She'd been sitting at the kitchen table, writing down words to the new cheer she'd just made up while her mother finished the dishes. She put her hand on her throat and felt that her glands were a little swollen. Every time she swallowed, it hurt, but she had too much on her mind to think about being sick.

She looked up from her notebook and drifted into a daydream about leading her squad to the state championship. The daydream didn't end there, however. Not only did her squad become the state champions, they went on to the nationals and became the champions of the entire country.

The best part of the daydream was that Heather

was disqualified from the squad because none of the judges liked her. When Jessica was being photographed and interviewed by dozens of journalists, Ken came running up to proclaim his love.

Jessica looked over to the crowd and saw the stricken Heather, sobbing her eyes out. . . .

"Jessica, honey," Mrs. Wakefield said. "Are you OK?"

"Yes, I'm fine," Jessica said, quickly snapping out of her daydream. "Why do you ask?"

"You've been coughing," Mrs. Wakefield said. "Maybe you're coming down with something."

"I'm as fit as a fiddle," Jessica said.

"Well, let's make sure you stay that way." Mrs. Wakefield put a vitamin-C tablet and a glass of water in front of Jessica on the table. "I want you to start taking vitamin C every four hours to make sure you don't get really sick."

"Mom, I'm not getting sick," Jessica groaned.

"Jessica . . ." Mrs. Wakefield warned.

"OK, OK," she said, gulping down the pill. *I guess the more vitamins, the better. After all, I need all my strength to lead us to the nationals! Sometimes dreams do come true!*

Chapter 8

"What's going on here?" Jessica asked Heather on Monday afternoon, her hands on her hips. "Practice isn't supposed to start for another ten minutes!"

"Oh, I thought I told Annie to tell you," Heather said, widening her eyes in an effort to look innocent.

"Tell me what?" Jessica fumed.

"I called practice for three thirty instead of four today," Heather said, smiling. "I thought we could use the extra half hour. The more time we spend practicing, the better we'll be. In fact, we should start practice earlier from now on."

"You're a *co*captain," Jessica said, shaking from head to toe. "It's not your job to make big decisions like that without consulting me first."

"I'm really sorry you weren't told about the change," Heather said. "I'll make sure it doesn't happen again. I was sure I told Annie to tell you, but I must have been mistaken."

"Jessica, look at these great pins Heather gave us," Helen said excitedly as she ran up to Jessica holding out a little pin in the shape of a cheerleading megaphone. "She gave one to each of us."

Jessica looked down at the miniature pin and wanted to rip it off Helen's shirt and throw it at Heather.

"Aren't they adorable?" Annie asked, beaming at Heather.

"What's the occasion?" Jessica asked, trying to remain calm.

"I just wanted to give the girls a little something to celebrate our new working relationship," Heather said. "Here's yours."

Jessica took the pin from Heather's palm and clasped it in her own. She walked away a few feet, and when nobody was looking, she threw it onto the ground and stomped it into the dirt with her sneaker. *That's what I think of your adorable little pin.*

"OK, I've worked out a really exciting new cheer that I think you're all going to love," Jessica said, trying to swallow her anger about Heather's starting practice without her and trying to buy the team's affection. "I want you all to watch closely while—"

Jessica turned around to face the girls and stopped in her tracks. They were all in some kind of formation, with Heather leading them.

"Jessica, look at this new cheer Heather was just in the middle of teaching us," Jeannie said. "I know you're going to love it."

"But I was just about to teach a new cheer," Jessica said. "I worked on it all weekend!"

"You go ahead and teach your little cheer," Heather said, moving to the side.

"But we were just in the middle of learning your cheer, Heather," Maria said. "It was just getting to the really fun part."

"Yeah, I want to know what comes next," Helen said. "I was really starting to feel like I was dancing instead of cheering."

"Jessica wants to teach her cheer," Heather said. "Maybe we can work on this one another time."

Jessica looked over at the girls, who had whiny, disappointed expressions on their faces.

"Please, Jessica," Jeannie pleaded. "Can't we just finish learning Heather's cheer? I promise you're going to love it."

"That's fine," Jessica said between clenched teeth. "Let's do Heather's cheer."

115

Jessica reluctantly moved into line with the rest of the squad. Even though she'd decided that she was going to show Heather who was in charge, she didn't want to make a big fuss about doing Heather's cheer instead of her own. After all, she didn't want Heather to have the satisfaction of thinking she was jealous of her.

Heather proceeded to teach her extremely complicated cheer, which was full of difficult steps.

"You all have to concentrate," Heather commanded them with a booming voice.

She sounds like a drill sergeant in the Marine Corps, Jessica thought. *Probably the girls will start hating her and change their minds about having her as their captain. Maybe I should just let her keep it up like this. Eventually, they'll be voting to kick her out of Sweet Valley and back to where she came from.*

"Sandy, you're moving around like a cow," Heather scolded. "Pretend like you're dancing. Try to have a little more fun with it. You really look ridiculous."

Jessica looked over at poor Sandy, who was huffing and puffing. Her face was bright red, and sweat was pouring down her face. Jessica got more and more excited as she realized that Heather would soon fall out of favor with the squad.

"Come on, Maria," Heather shouted. "You're not getting it. Watch me."

116

Heather did her stupid cheer and made it look totally effortless. *Of course it's easy for her. She's the one who made it up,* Jessica thought.

"Maria, put some effort into it," Heather scolded. "You really have to work harder than that. This isn't going to cut it on a national level."

"I'm trying, Heather," Maria said, practically in tears.

"I want to see you girls sweat," Heather said. "There's no way our football team will win if you get out on the field with that kind of low energy."

And there's no way you're going to win "most favored captain" if you keep yelling at everyone like that, Jessica thought gleefully.

"That was a great dinner," Elizabeth said to Todd. "Your mom's such a good cook."

It was Tuesday night, and Elizabeth and Todd were sitting in the Wilkinses' den on the couch. Their schoolbooks were next to them, but they hadn't cracked them open yet.

"Mom's the best cook in Sweet Valley," Todd said proudly, pulling Elizabeth closer to him. "They love it when you come over. I think Mom and Dad love you almost as much as I do, if that's possible."

"I love them too," Elizabeth said. "Your dad's hysterical. I know where you got your sense of humor."

"Yeah, he's a pretty crazy guy," Todd said, moving even closer to Elizabeth. "And you're making *me* crazy right now." Todd started to kiss Elizabeth passionately on the lips.

"Hey, I thought we were supposed to be studying," Elizabeth said, wriggling away.

"I'm studying you," Todd said, whispering in her ear.

Elizabeth wiped her ear with her hand. The sweeter Todd was being, the more he was bothering her. The last thing she felt like doing was fooling around.

"Come on, I have a lot of homework to do." Elizabeth slid away from Todd on the couch and opened up her American-history book.

"You've been more studious than usual lately," Todd said, sliding back toward her. "I mean, I know you're a serious student and everything, but usually you still have time to have fun."

"I guess I just have more work these days," Elizabeth said quickly. "Work that I have to do *now*."

"OK, I'll try to control myself, but it's not going to be easy," Todd said, opening his calculus book. "You're irresistible tonight. I love what you're wearing."

Elizabeth looked down to see what was so special about what she was wearing. She had on a pair of blue jeans and a pink cotton T-shirt. Her hair was pulled back in a white headband, and she wasn't wearing makeup. *He certainly is easy to please,* she thought, somehow annoyed by the fact.

They both read their books for about five minutes; then Todd closed his book and grabbed Elizabeth's.

"What do you think you're doing?" Elizabeth asked.

"Taking a study break," Todd said, kissing her neck.

Elizabeth closed her eyes and let Todd continue to kiss her. It felt good at first, but suddenly, before she knew it, she had replaced Todd in her mind's eye with Ken.

"What's wrong?" Todd asked.

"I thought you said we were going to study," Elizabeth said angrily. "I came over here because I thought I'd get some work done, but you're making that impossible." Elizabeth hated the way her voice sounded. Todd looked like a wounded puppy dog. *Why am I being so mean to him?*

"I thought you came over to see me and have dinner with my parents," Todd said sadly. "I'm sorry you're not having a good time. Are you mad at me about something? I mean, besides trying to kiss you?"

Elizabeth was consumed with guilt. But instead of being nicer to Todd because of her guilt, she just seemed to get meaner and meaner. She was mad at herself, but she was taking it out on poor Todd, who had no idea what was going on.

"I'm not mad at you about anything," Elizabeth said, hating herself. "I think I should just go home." Before Todd could say anything, Elizabeth was on her way out the door. *I'm going to destroy this relationship if I keep acting like this,* Elizabeth thought. *How much more will Todd be able to take of my weird behavior?*

What are those two talking about? Jessica wondered as she walked up the front steps of school on Wednesday morning and saw Lila standing with Heather.

"Thanks for last night," Lila was saying to Heather. "That was a blast."

"I'm so glad you guys came," Heather said. "We'll have to do it again soon."

"Good morning, Jessica," Heather said cheerfully. "You're looking really pretty today."

And you're acting as fake and two-faced as ever, Jessica felt like saying.

Jessica noticed that Lila suddenly looked uncomfortable. She blushed slightly and started twirling a strand of her long brown hair with her finger.

"Hi, Jessica," Lila muttered. "I didn't see you come up the stairs."

"Are you ready for the big game this afternoon?" Heather asked Jessica.

"As ready as ever," Jessica said energetically. *And ready to show you that you can't push around Jessica Wakefield,* she thought.

"I'll see you guys later," Heather said as she hurried into the school.

Jessica turned to look at Lila, who was avoiding eye contact with her. "What were you two talking about?" Jessica asked suspiciously.

"I forgot," Lila said nervously. "I'm sure it was nothing interesting. We need to go inside. We're going to be late for homeroom."

"I don't care if we miss homeroom all together," Jessica said. "You were saying something to Heather about last night. You said whatever it was was a blast."

"Oh, right," Lila said, obviously pretending as if she were just then remembering what they'd been talking about. "A couple of us went over to Heather's last night for dinner," she said quickly.

For a minute Jessica thought she must have heard Lila incorrectly. It couldn't be possible that her best friend went to Heather's house. Could it? "Can you be a little more specific? Who went there and why?"

"Annie, Amy, and a couple of guys and I went

121

over to her house," Lila said. "She had a little dinner party. Sort of a 'get acquainted' thing."

"What guys?" Jessica asked.

"Barry, Bruce, Rick, and Ken," Lila almost whispered the last name.

"Ken Matthews?" Jessica asked in disbelief. "What did you guys do? How could you go there? Why didn't she invite me?"

"Calm down," Lila said. "It was really nothing. We just ate dinner out by her pool. Apparently, at her old school she and her friends used to give dinner parties all the time. She wanted to do that here. And as for your not being invited, she talked to me about that."

"I'm dying to know what she had to say," Jessica fumed.

"She said she would have loved to have invited you, but she had the feeling you didn't really like her," Lila explained.

"Gee, I wonder how she got that idea," Jessica asked sarcastically.

"I'm sorry you didn't come. You would have had a good time. Her house is amazing. It's almost as big as mine, and she has a tennis court like I do."

"Well, I'm sure she's really sorry I wasn't there," Jessica said, getting more agitated by the minute.

"She was," Lila insisted. "She's upset that you

don't like her. She even asked me if I would put in a good word for her because she'd like to be your friend."

"That'll be the day," Jessica said. "How could you go to her party? You're supposed to be my best friend and you know I don't like Heather. You could have shown some loyalty."

"Just because you don't like somebody doesn't mean I can't like them," Lila said. "You and I are still best buddies, but we don't have to have all the same friends."

"You honestly like Heather?" Jessica asked.

"Yes, I do," Lila said. "And I think you'd like her too if you'd just give her a chance. She's really cool. She made a fabulous dinner, and she really created a cool ambience, with candles and everything. She's very sophisticated."

"Excuse me while I throw up," Jessica said. It was truly amazing to her that even her best friend was being seduced by the fake charms of her enemy. "So tell me what Ken was like last night."

"There's not much to tell," Lila said.

"Come on, how did he act with Heather? Were they flirting? Did they sit next to each other at dinner?"

"They did sit next to each other, but it didn't look like anything was really going on between

123

them," Lila said. "They were just being friendly."

"How friendly?" Jessica asked.

"You're starting to sound paranoid," Lila said. "You have nothing to worry about. He asked *you* out for Friday night, not Heather. Now, can we please go to homeroom? We're already five minutes late."

Jessica walked into the school feeling lousy. *It's not enough that Heather has to try to steal my squad—now she's trying to steal my new boyfriend and my best friend!*

"Sweet success!" Heather yelled at the top of her lungs, leading the cheerleaders in her victory cheer. Then she jumped on top of the pyramid the cheerleaders had made, and the crowd went wild. It was Wednesday afternoon, and the Gladiators had just beaten Whitman in an overtime game.

Every time Jessica had started to lead a cheer, Heather had practically jumped in front of her and started off on one of her own. And what made it worse was that she'd choreographed practically every cheer so that it featured her. At the end of the cheers Heather would finish it off with a splashy flip or running splits.

The worst part was that the fans seemed to love Heather and her routines. Jessica didn't think she'd ever heard them respond to the cheering squad so enthusiastically. She was in a terrible mood.

"That was amazing," Lila said to the girls after the game.

"Your squad has never been so good," Winston Egbert exclaimed. "I thought the bleachers were going to collapse—the fans were going wild!"

Yes, we have been this good, Jessica wanted to say. *We were ten times this good two Fridays ago before anyone even knew who Heather Mallone was!*

Even though Heather had once again stolen the spotlight, Jessica took some comfort in the fact that she was still cocaptain and their squad was getting a lot of attention. Jessica would at least get some of the credit for their strong performance.

Jessica saw a handsome reporter from the local newspaper coming toward her with a notebook and pen. "I understand you're the captain of the cheerleading squad," he said to Jessica. "I was wondering if you could answer a few questions about the new cheers you were doing out there today. You were certainly a crowd pleaser."

"Actually, I'm the person who made up all those cheers," Heather said, jumping right in front of Jessica.

"And what's your name?" the reporter asked eagerly.

"Heather Mallone. I'm one of the cocaptains. I'm new to Sweet Valley."

Jessica was so livid she couldn't even speak. She just stood there with her mouth open.

"How long have you been here?" the reporter asked.

"Just a little over a week," Heather said in that annoying, flirtatious voice Jessica had heard before.

"What a great story," the reporter said. "In just one week you've come to town and turned this squad around. I have to go to a lot of football and basketball games for my job, and I must say, I've never seen better cheerleaders."

"Why, thank you," Heather gushed. "It's going to take a while to really get these girls into shape, but we're off to a good start. Rome wasn't built in a day, after all."

Rome wasn't built in a day! Jessica repeated in her head. That was about the dumbest thing she'd ever heard. How dare Heather put down the squad like that to a reporter? This was the last straw. *From now on it's back to the Jessica Wakefield way of doing things,* Jessica decided as she stormed off the field.

Chapter 9

"That's really turned into a nasty cough," Mrs. Wakefield said to Jessica on Thursday morning at breakfast. "And you don't look well at all."

"I'm fine," Jessica said, though the truth was that she was feeling lousy. Her throat was so sore, she couldn't bear even to swallow her orange juice. "I'm probably just coughing from yelling so much at the game yesterday."

"Your squad did a great job," Elizabeth said. "As you know, I don't usually pay much attention to cheerleading, but I did notice that the crowds were more enthusiastic than usual at yesterday's game. You must be really proud."

"Don't you go jumping on the Heather bandwagon along with everyone else," Jessica said. "I'll really be in trouble if my own sister sides with her."

"What are you talking about?" Elizabeth asked.

"Let's just say that yesterday was the Heather Mallone show," Jessica said. "She took all the credit for the work the squad's been doing all year. She's only been in Sweet Valley for a little over one week."

"Jessica, your cheeks are all flushed!" Mrs. Wakefield said. "I think you're running a temperature."

"Don't worry, Mom," Jessica insisted. "I just turn red whenever I talk about Heather."

Mrs. Wakefield felt Jessica's forehead with the back of her hand and shook her head. "You're burning up. I don't even need a thermometer to tell me that you're running a temperature."

"It's just hot in here," Jessica said, even though she was feeling chilled, the way she always did when she had a fever.

"No, it isn't," Mr. Wakefield said, looking over the top of his newspaper. "It's actually a little cool in here."

"You have a fever, and you're staying home from school today," Mrs. Wakefield said.

"Jessica, you're usually thrilled to stay home from school," Elizabeth pointed out. "You can watch your silly soap operas all day."

"I can't stay home from school today," Jessica protested. "It's out of the question."

"I'm sorry, but this isn't open for discussion,"

Mrs. Wakefield said. "There's no way you're going to school today, and that's that. Elizabeth, honey, could you pass me the marmalade, please?"

"You don't understand," Jessica pleaded. "I can't let that horrible Heather person lead practice this afternoon without me. She's trying to take over the squad, and she's about to succeed."

"You do look pretty rotten, Jessica," Elizabeth said. "And I heard you coughing for most of the night last night."

"But I feel perfectly fine," Jessica said, annoyed with her sister. "It's not fair."

"You can watch TV all day long," Mrs. Wakefield said. "And I'll even make you a nice fruit salad before I go to work."

"And I'll bring you home a hot-fudge sundae from the Dairi Burger on my way home from school," Elizabeth offered.

"I guess I don't have any say in this," Jessica said.

"You're right. You don't," Mr. Wakefield said.

"Feel better," Elizabeth said, leaping up from the table. "I'll see you later."

"Thanks for nothing," Jessica yelled after her. "You've succeeded in helping to ruin my day!"

Elizabeth sat on the bleachers on Thursday afternoon watching football practice. She was not a football fan, and she should have been in the *Oracle* office working on an article, but there was something she had to do that was more important.

Number seventy-five. That was Ken's number. Even though he was wearing a helmet, Elizabeth couldn't keep her eyes off him. His great personality was evident even at a distance. He was making the other players laugh, and when one of the guys fumbled the ball, Ken put his arm around him, reassuring him that it was OK.

She felt bad about helping to convince her mother that Jessica should stay home from school that day, but she knew it would give her a chance to talk to Ken without Jessica's getting in the way. *If Jessica's still sick tomorrow, she won't be able to go on her second date with Ken,* she thought hopefully. It was awful to wish for her sister's ill health, but she just couldn't help it.

Elizabeth didn't even know what she was going to say to Ken. Maybe if she just spent some time alone with him, she'd be able to tell what her true feelings were. She also wanted to find out what his feelings were for her.

Just watching him during the practice made her remember how much she used to like him. But was it just the memory of their time together that she was holding on to? If Todd had never come back from Vermont and they'd continued to see each other, would things have ended naturally? Would they still be together now? Would Ken be interested in Jessica?

Maybe I should just leave now, Elizabeth thought as practice ended. *No,* she thought resolutely, *I have to settle this once and for all.*

When practice was over, Elizabeth walked down to the field and waited for Ken to come by on his way to the locker room.

"Ken!"

Ken was undoing the hook of his helmet and taking it off when he turned around and saw Elizabeth. He looked surprised and startled. His face was all red from practicing, and his blond hair was matted down from the helmet, but he looked more handsome than ever.

"Elizabeth," he said under his breath. "What are you doing here? Todd's not here, if you're looking for him." Ken looked off into the distance, averting his eyes from Elizabeth.

Just hearing Todd's name made her feel guilty, and all the things she wanted to say to Ken escaped her. He looked more nervous to see Elizabeth than she was to see him. This was a bad idea, she thought, suddenly feeling very foolish.

"Do you know where he is?" Elizabeth asked. She knew she sounded cold and distant, but she couldn't help it.

"No. No idea," Ken muttered.

"OK, thanks," Elizabeth quickly said, then rushed off, feeling ridiculous.

"Elizabeth?" Ken yelled after her.

Elizabeth stopped and turned around. Her heart was pounding. *This is it,* she thought. *The moment I've been waiting for. He's going to tell me now that he's really not interested in Jessica but he's just trying to get to me, or that he's still in love with me but he can't hurt his best friend.*

"Yes?" Elizabeth asked, holding her breath.

"Uh, say hi to Jessica for me," he said awkwardly, almost as if that wasn't what he had intended to say. "Tell her I hope she feels better."

Ken's words stung her ears. "Sure thing," she practically whispered, and turned back around.

He doesn't care about me at all, she thought as she walked off the field. *He acted like nothing had ever happened between us. Like all the kissing and laughing and late-night talks never happened. So I have to forget him, too. That's exactly what I have to do—forget what we shared and just concentrate on Todd. As hard as it's going to be, I have to let him go.*

Chapter 10

It was Thursday afternoon, and Jessica was lying on the couch in the family room watching her favorite soap opera, *The Bold and the Beautiful*. She'd been watching television all day. She was feeling a little groggy and sleepy, and as much as she loved her soaps, she was starting to get bored.

She looked at the digital clock on the VCR and saw that cheerleading practice was probably over. What a relief. She hated thinking about Heather leading the girls without her. The big game was in only two days, and she was determined not to let Heather steal the show the way she had at the last game. *Heather's moment in the sun is over,* Jessica thought as the cordless phone that was right next to her on the couch started ringing.

133

"Hello," Jessica said into the receiver as she hit the mute button on the remote control. She heard someone crying on the other line, but she couldn't tell who it was or what they were saying. "Who is this?"

"Jessica, it's Maria," she said between small sobs.

"Maria? What's wrong? Are you hurt? Where are you?"

"I'm OK physically but . . ." Her voice trailed off.

"OK, take a deep breath and tell me what's going on," Jessica instructed her calmly.

After a long silence Maria finally spoke. "It's Heather."

Jessica bristled at the mention of the name. "What has she done *now*?"

"She kicked Sandy and me off the squad," Maria blurted out. "I feel so terrible. I love being a cheerleader. It's so embarrassing. I never want to show my face in school again. Nobody gets kicked off the cheering squad. I feel like a total loser."

"Slow down!" Jessica sat up straight and threw the remote control she was holding onto the floor. "Heather kicked you off the squad? Start from the beginning."

"Heather said we just weren't working hard enough and that we'd make everyone else look bad in the routines. She said that everyone had to be at the same level or else there was no point in having a cheering squad at all."

"But she can't do that!" Jessica felt her temperature going up a degree every second.

"She already did it," Maria cried.

"You and Sandy are great cheerleaders, and all the girls on the squad agree. I'm sure they must have put up a strong protest."

"That's the worst part," Maria said, sniffling. "They all stood by Heather's decision. I thought they were my friends, but I guess I was wrong."

"They *are* your friends," Jessica said. "It doesn't make sense. Why would they side with Heather against you guys? They barely even know her."

"Heather's convinced them that if they do everything she says, they'll make it to the nationals. She gave this whole speech about how when she saw our squad for the first time at the Big Mesa game, she didn't think we stood a chance of even making it to the state finals."

"But we were better than ever at the Big Mesa game," Jessica cried. *And that was the last time that I was really in control of the squad,* Jessica thought, remembering how happy she'd been after that game.

"She said that after Wednesday's game, she realized that we actually had some potential," Maria said.

"Of course she'd say that. That's when she was jumping in front of everyone and making it *her* squad," Jessica said bitterly.

"She said the squad had to make sacrifices if they wanted to get anywhere, and that if Sandy and I stayed on the squad, we'd hold them back."

"So she sacrificed you and Sandy! That girl has some nerve!"

"You don't think I'm a bad cheerleader, do you?" Maria asked, then started to cry even harder.

"Of course not," Jessica said. She was suddenly more awake and clearheaded than ever. "This is just another one of her ways to try to take control away from me. Don't worry, I'm not going to let her get away with this!"

"Who do you think you are?" Jessica yelled at Heather on Friday morning. Heather was standing at her locker, and Jessica slammed it shut.

"I don't understand the question," Heather said calmly. She smiled at Jessica as if her behavior were perfectly normal.

"I see through that fake sweetness act that everybody else is buying, so you can lose that stupid smile."

"I'm afraid I don't know what you're talking about," Heather said with an innocent expression on her face.

"You know exactly what I'm talking about," Jessica said. "You have no right to fire people from the squad without consulting me first. What you did yesterday was completely out of line, and you're not getting away with it."

"Oh, you mean letting Sandy and Maria go," Heather said, pushing a strand of curly hair behind her ear.

"Sandy and Maria were on the squad long before you arrived in Sweet Valley, and they're going to be on it long after you're gone," Jessica said. She hadn't let off steam like that in a long time, and it actually felt good. Speaking her mind—especially when someone had crossed her—was one of the things she did best.

"Relax, Jessica," Heather said smugly. "You're getting yourself way too worked up. You don't want to make yourself sick again."

"Don't tell me to relax," Jessica said. Jessica hated being told to relax, especially by someone she couldn't stand. "I would never have given approval for you to kick Maria and Sandy off the squad."

"Your loyalty is really sweet, but even *you* have to admit that those girls just aren't up to speed," Heather said. "They were really an embarrassment to the squad."

"That's the most ridiculous thing I've ever heard,"

Jessica fumed. "They're both fantastic cheerleaders, and besides, that's not even the point."

"What *is* the point?" Heather asked impatiently as if she were late for an important appointment.

"The point is that you can't do something like that on your own without talking to me about it first," Jessica said.

"Actually, you're wrong about that," Heather said. "According to the guidelines and regulations of the Sweet Valley cheerleading rule book, if one captain is gone, the other captain has the authority to make any decision she sees fit at the time."

Heather pulled out the book and opened it to the page she was referring to.

"I've never seen this before," Jessica said, reading the page. "And besides, I was only gone for one practice."

"Sorry, but it doesn't matter if you were gone for one day or one month," Heather said, shaking her head. "You weren't there when I made the decision, and it's too late for you to do anything about it."

"I'm sure none of the other girls are going to go along with this, and you're not going to have much of a squad if everyone quits," Jessica said.

"Go ahead and talk to the other girls on the squad. They all agree with me."

"You haven't heard the last of this," Jessica

said, throwing the rule book at Heather's feet. "You're going to be sorry you ever set foot in this school."

"I'll see you at practice, Jessica," Heather said, turning on her heel to walk away. "Oh, and try not to be late again. Toodles!"

OK, this is war! Jessica thought as she stood trembling with anger. *Those girls are coming back on our squad, and Heather is going to be history!* Jessica felt sure that if she just talked rationally to the rest of the squad, they'd all stand by her. *It's Wakefield against Mallone now!*

"That's really rotten about getting cut from the cheering squad," Winston said to Maria on Friday. They were eating lunch with Elizabeth and Todd, and the lunchroom was buzzing with excitement as everyone talked about their weekend plans.

"I still can't believe it," Maria said. "When I went to practice yesterday, that was the last thing I expected to happen."

"That Heather Mallone seems like trouble," Elizabeth had to admit. She hated to see her friend so upset even if it *was* about cheerleading. She knew how important it was to her—almost as important as it was to Jessica. "I know my sister really doesn't like her."

"Jessica's been great," Maria said. "She's as upset about all this as I am."

"With her on your side, I'm sure you'll be back on the squad in no time," Elizabeth consoled. "She almost always gets what she wants, and I know she wants you back on the squad."

"I hope you're right," Maria said, smiling weakly.

"Speaking of Jessica, I understand she and Ken have a big date tonight," Todd said. "Ken told me he'd planned something very romantic."

Elizabeth dropped her tuna sandwich onto her plate. *Don't get upset,* she told herself. *Remember, you decided to let Ken go.*

"They make a great couple," Winston said. "They really look like they go together."

And since I look just like Jessica, I guess we look like we go together as well, Elizabeth thought.

"Ken seems to be really nuts about Jessica," Todd said, putting his arm around Elizabeth. "I don't think I've ever seen him get so excited about a girl before."

Elizabeth couldn't help wondering if he'd been as excited about her as he was about Jessica. As much as she was trying not to get upset, those familiar jealous feelings were creeping up again. She had a flashback to the day before, when she'd tried to talk to Ken at the football field. He wouldn't look at her, and she felt as if she were talking to a complete stranger. Suddenly she was overcome with a heavy sadness, and she knew she wouldn't be able to sit through the rest of the meal.

"Excuse me, but I have to go do something," Elizabeth said, standing up from the table.

"Are you OK?" Todd asked. "Do you want me to come with you?"

"I'm fine," Elizabeth said. "I'll see you later."

Elizabeth rushed out of the lunchroom and out the front door of the school. She sat down on the grass and closed her eyes. It was impossible. As hard as she'd tried, she couldn't shake Ken out of her system.

"Jeannie, I'm using your brush," Jessica said as she flipped her head over and brushed it underneath. "I must have left mine in my locker."

It was Friday afternoon, and Jessica, Lila, and some of the girls from the cheerleading squad were in the school bathroom, primping between classes. Every Friday they usually convened in the bathroom at the same time. Since it was the start of the weekend, they made an extra effort to look their best. This was an especially big weekend, since the big football game was the next day and Lila was having a party that night after the game.

Jessica thought this was the perfect time to plead her case against Heather. She decided to do it calmly, presenting a rational argument in favor of keeping Maria and Sandy on the team rather than insulting Heather. She knew that the squad was totally blinded by Heather's charms, so she had to proceed cautiously. She had to wait for the right moment and bring it up in a subtle way.

"Who's got my new lipstick?" Helen asked.

"I have it," Annie said as she rubbed her lips together and studied them in the mirror. "I don't think it's my color, though."

"You're right," Lila said, pausing in the middle of applying mascara. "You look like Joan Crawford. Wipe it off and try mine. It's less harsh."

"Is it true that you're having a band at your party tomorrow night?" Amy asked Lila.

"Yeah, it's going to be great," Lila said. "They're a band from Los Angeles, and they just cut a new CD."

"I can't wait," Jeannie said.

"Are you excited about your date tonight with Ken?" Jeannie asked Jessica.

"I'm totally excited," Jessica said. Just thinking about it gave Jessica goose bumps and made her feel a little bit better after her ugly scene with Heather. "But I'm still upset about Heather's firing Maria and Sandy yesterday while I was gone."

"I guess she felt like she had to do it," Annie said. "She really seems to think we have a chance to go to the nationals. She just didn't think we'd make it with Sandy and Maria dragging us down."

"What do you all think?" Jessica asked. "I mean, Sandy and Maria are your friends. Do *you* think they're dragging down the team?"

"I don't know," Helen said sheepishly. "Maybe she's right."

"Heather seems to really know what she's doing," Jeannie said. "She's had a lot more experience in these things than I have, so I guess I trust her decision."

"But she's only been here a couple of weeks," Jessica said. "She doesn't know our school *or* our squad, and you don't know *her*. Most of you have known Maria and Sandy practically forever. How can you turn your backs on them?"

"Let's face it," Jeannie said. "We really want the chance to go to the nationals, and it seems like Heather will be able to take us there."

"Jeannie, who is your very best friend in the whole world?" Jessica asked, knowing very well what the answer was.

"Sandy's my best friend," Jeannie practically whispered.

"Exactly," Jessica said. "Sandy's your best

143

friend, yet you're willing to just forget about your friendship because of some person who just rode into town in a Mazda Miata telling you you can make it to the nationals."

"Jessica, I would think that you of all people would be excited to go to the nationals," Amy said, pulling her hair back in a headband. "After all, you've said in the past that going to the nationals would be a dream come true."

"It *would* be a dream come true if we did it the right way," Jessica said.

"You mean if we did it *your* way," Jeannie said.

"You guys are totally blinded by that girl's big promises," Jessica said. "She's fooled all of you. She's nothing but a self-centered, conniving troublemaker, but you can't see past all the flashy talk about the nationals and those stupid little pins she gave you." Jessica just couldn't keep the insults from flying out of her mouth. She'd tried it the other way, but it wasn't working. *Maybe tough talk is the only way to get through to these people*, Jessica thought.

"I happen to like Heather," Helen said.

"So do I," Jeannie said.

"Me too," Annie said.

"If I didn't know better, I'd say you were just jealous of Heather," Amy said.

"Jealous?" Jessica gasped. "Me, jealous of someone as two-faced and rude as Heather Mallone? I hope you're kidding. That's the second time you've said that to me, Amy, and I hope it's the last. Nothing could be further from the truth."

"I just think it would be really selfish of you to deny the rest of us a chance to follow our dream just because you have a personal problem with the one person who can help us," Amy said.

She's brainwashed them! Jessica thought, mortified. She felt as if some horrible conspiracy were going on that she couldn't stop. *How can all these girls be so mean to their friends? How can they buy into Heather's phoniness?*

"I'll see you guys at practice," Jessica said on her way out of the bathroom. "And I hope you'll think long and hard about what I've said here. Just imagine how you'd feel if you were Maria or Sandy. Think how it would be to have all your friends forget about you—and about all the hard work you'd put into cheering over the year." Jessica slammed the door behind her, feeling lonelier than she'd ever felt before.

Chapter 11

"Hey, Jessica, you look like you just found out you have six months to live," Lila said.

"That's exactly how I feel," Jessica groaned. She was sitting by herself under a tree on the front lawn of the school, holding her head in her hands. It was almost time for cheerleading practice, but Jessica didn't want to go. After that awful talk she'd had earlier in the day with the girls on the squad, she felt defeated.

Normally, she'd try to find her sister at a time like that, but Elizabeth had been acting so distant lately. Every time Jessica started to talk about Ken—the only thing that had been giving her any pleasure in the last couple of weeks—Elizabeth had to make some negative comment. She felt too far away from her to confide her feelings.

She didn't even feel like talking to Lila. After all, Lila seemed to be as big a fan of Heather's as everyone else was.

"If you don't mind, I think I want to be left alone," Jessica said, lying down on her back.

Lila, obviously choosing to ignore Jessica's wishes, sat down next to her and plucked a blade of grass, which she wrapped around her fingers. "You were great today with those girls. You really stood up for Maria and Sandy. And I want you to know that if I were on the squad, I'd be on your side."

Jessica looked at her friend and felt a flood of warm emotions. Even though Lila could be a real pain sometimes, she always came through when it really mattered. "Thanks, Lila. That really means a lot to me. I wish you *were* on the squad."

"And I agree with you about Heather," Lila said, lying down and looking up at the sky.

"You do? I thought you liked her," Jessica said. "Just the other day you were saying how cool and sophisticated you thought she was."

"Yeah, I guess I thought so at first," Lila said. "She can certainly be charming when she wants to be."

"What made you change your mind?"

"The more I've been watching her, the more I'm seeing her true personality," Lila said. "I think that it was really rotten of her to fire Maria and Sandy from the team. And I think the way she's been competing with you and turning the girls on the squad against you is the lowest."

"You have no idea how happy that makes me to hear you say that," Jessica said. "I've been feeling like I'm on a totally different planet from everyone else. Like I'm the only one that could see Heather for what she really is."

"You're not the only one," Lila said. "I think she's sneaky and selfish."

"Why can't anyone else see that?"

"People just see what they want to see when they think they can gain something," Lila said. "Those girls really want to go to the championships, and they honestly believe Heather can take them there. I know it's hard, but you can't really blame them for wanting that. It's just too bad they're turning their backs on you and their other friends."

"I guess you're right," Jessica said. "But it doesn't help. Heather's managed to turn the one thing I love more than almost anything into a nightmare."

Lila looked at her watch. "Shouldn't you be getting ready for practice?"

"I don't think I'm up to it," Jessica said glumly. "What's the point? Heather has them totally in her camp. I thought for sure that when she fired Maria and Sandy, they'd see Heather for what she really is. Obviously, I was wrong. I don't know what else I can say that I haven't already said."

"Excuse me, but what have you done with Jessica Wakefield?" Lila teased. "The Jessica I know would be marching onto that football field, demanding that Maria and Sandy be put back on the squad."

Jessica felt a sudden surge of energy. "You're right! I'm not going to sit here and let Heather destroy the lives of my squad members, and I'm not going to let her take my squad away from me! I've fought bigger battles than this one, and I'm not going to let Heather get me down!"

"Now, that's the Jessica I know," Lila said, sitting up.

Jessica jumped up on her feet. "I'm going to march onto that field like you said, and I'm going to give them an ultimatum—either Maria and Sandy are back on the squad, or I'm off it for good!"

"Three cheers for Jessica Wakefield!" Lila shouted as she stood up and did a cartwheel.

"Hey, not bad!" Jessica said. "Maybe you should be on the squad."

"I think you have enough problems as it is," Lila teased.

"Speaking of problems, Heather Mallone, hear I come!" Jessica ran as fast as she could to the locker room to get ready for practice.

Jessica was out of breath by the time she reached the far end of the football field. The girls were standing around talking and stretching before practice. Jessica was feeling stronger and more determined than ever after her talk with Lila, and she was ready to deliver her ultimatum to the squad. She looked around the field, but Heather was nowhere in sight.

My timing couldn't be more perfect, Jessica thought with excitement. *She'll be surprised when she shows up and finds out that the squad has stood by me.*

"Excuse me," Jessica yelled to the girls. "I need to talk to all of you about something really important. As you know, yesterday Heather—"

"Oh, hi, girls!" Heather shouted from behind Jessica. "Sorry I'm late. I was picking up these new uniforms."

Jessica turned around and saw Heather carrying two big cardboard boxes. As soon as Heather dropped the boxes onto the ground, all the girls crowded around them. They pulled out the new red-and-white uniforms, one by one.

Jessica looked at the uniforms as the girls

held them up for inspection. She was actually pleased. They were so hideous looking that Jessica was sure the other girls would hate them. The skirts were supershort with fringe around the bottom, and the shirts were skimpy little tank tops. *Fine. Maybe I won't even have to give an ultimatum,* Jessica thought. *They'll be so disgusted by Heather's uniforms that they won't want her to have anything to do with the squad.*

"These are *fabulous,*" Amy gushed.

"They don't even look like uniforms," Jeannie exclaimed. "I would wear this to a party."

"They're totally sexy," Annie said, holding one of the shirts up to her chest. "These will really get us some attention."

"Our other uniforms are so boring compared to these," Helen said.

Jessica couldn't believe what she was hearing. *How could anyone think those ugly things are fabulous? Has Heather brainwashed them so much that they now have her same tacky taste?*

"First of all, you and I never had a discussion about new uniforms," Jessica said to Heather. "And second of all, we can't afford these. Our budget is low as it is."

"They're a gift from me," Heather said, beaming. "I couldn't bear seeing these gorgeous girls wearing those drab, juvenile uniforms anymore.

They looked like children in those things."

"I chose those uniforms," Jessica said, clenching her fists tightly.

"Maybe Jessica's right," Heather said to the girls. "Why don't you put those back in the boxes? You should stick with Jessica's uniforms. After all, she was your captain before I came along."

"No way!" Amy protested. "We want these new ones. Don't we, girls?"

"Yes!" everybody shouted at the same time.

Jessica was once again humiliated by Heather. *She set me up,* Jessica thought. *She tried to make me look like the bad guy. Why can't anyone else see that?*

"Sorry, Jessica, but it looks like they want to go with my uniforms," Heather said. "I guess that's just the way the cookie crumbles."

Jessica was too angry to speak; she just glared at Heather with a hateful expression.

"Now I want everyone to sit around in a circle," Heather commanded.

Jessica stood to the side, refusing to sit down in Heather's stupid circle.

"Uniforms alone are not going to get us to the nationals," Heather said, pulling out a stack of papers from her knapsack. "It doesn't matter how great you look out there. If you're not in shape, you're not worth diddly."

"Jessica, could you pass these around?" Heather asked, handing Jessica the pile of papers.

"No, I couldn't pass them around," Jessica said curtly, taking one of the pages for herself. She was curious to see what else Heather was up to.

"That's fine," Heather said sweetly. "Who *would* like to pass these around?"

"I would," Amy volunteered.

Jessica looked down at the piece of paper in her hand. It contained a daily diet-and-exercise regime that looked like something designed for a labor camp.

"Oh, Jessica, I didn't consult you about this, but I'm sure you want the squad to go to the nationals as much as I do," Heather said, smiling sweetly at Jessica.

Jessica looked around the circle at the expectant faces waiting for her reaction. *I'm not going to let her set me up again,* Jessica decided. *She's turned them against me enough as it is.*

"That's just fine," Jessica said, smiling back at Heather with the same syrupy smile.

"Great. As you'll see on the handout, I've put together a program that everyone on the squad has to follow," Heather said. "It's going to seem hard at first, but you'll realize that it's worth it. Every girl on this squad is expected to jog three miles a day. This is something you're going to have to do on your own time. If it means waking up an hour earlier every day, then so be it."

They're going to be running right off this field and straight to the Dairi Burger by the time she's done with this stupid diet-and-exercise nonsense.

"In addition to jogging, you're all going to have to lift weights for an hour a day," Heather said. "There are weights in the gym, and I have a Nautilus machine at my house, which you're all free to use whenever you want."

"That's so generous of you," Jeannie said.

"Not at all," Heather said as if she were Mother Teresa. "I'm happy to do anything for this squad that I possibly can to help you get to the nationals."

Jessica, who was about ready to throw up, was trying as hard as she could to keep her mouth shut and let Heather dig her own grave. She couldn't believe that nobody had protested yet about the exercise, but she knew it was only a matter of time.

"At the beginning of every practice, we're going to start with seventy-five sit-ups, thirty push-ups, and fifty jumping jacks." Heather paused and looked around the circle. "I know I'm asking a lot, so if anyone wants to get off this bus now, this is the moment."

Jessica held her breath as she waited to hear the first person say she didn't want to do Heather's stupid exercises, but nobody said a word. *Wait until she gets to this diet plan,* Jessica thought, looking down at her paper. *That'll scare them.*

"OK, then, let's proceed to the diet portion of the regime," Heather said. "In order to achieve the perfect, healthy body, we have to combine exercise with diet. I want you to start thinking right now that fat is your enemy. You're all going on a strict no-fat diet. If I hear of anyone eating any fat, they're off the squad. That means you can only have skim milk in your coffee, and obviously milk shakes are out of the question. If you must eat pizza, ask to have it without cheese. I do it all the time."

Pizza without cheese? Jessica had never heard of anything so ridiculous. *They'll never go for this!*

"You can eat as many fruits, vegetables, and grains as you want," Heather said. "That's all I ever eat, and I never feel deprived."

"You do have a fantastic figure," Amy gushed. "I guess this plan really works. I'd kill for a body like yours."

Oh, great. Heather really needs people to tell her what a great body she has, as if her ego weren't already big enough, Jessica thought.

"I want you to keep in mind that this is not

about having a great body for vanity purposes," Heather said. "The idea is that your bodies will be stronger than ever and therefore able to do the different cheers and steps that will be required. The better the body, the better the cheerleader. You'll see that I've written down a typical day of eating. You can start with one half of a grapefruit for breakfast and a big glass of water. For lunch you can have any kind of vegetables that you want as long as you don't put anything on them. You can even eat rice with your vegetables as long as it's brown rice. For dinner you can have a salad, but you have to use lemon juice for your dressing. Oh, and in the afternoon you can have a piece of fruit or a carrot stick."

Jessica started laughing out loud in spite of herself.

"What's so funny, Jessica?" Heather asked. "Did we miss a joke?"

"I'm just laughing at this diet plan," Jessica said. "There's no way these people are going to go along with it. I mean, get real, pizza without cheese?" Jessica looked at all the girls, expecting them to smile at her in agreement, but they all just looked at her as if she were a complete stranger.

"Maybe this *is* too severe," Heather said. "Would you all like to just forget about this whole thing and go back to the way things were before I became a cocaptain? You probably won't even make it to the state finals, but maybe that's what you want. Obviously, that's what Jessica wants."

Nobody said a word, and Jessica was starting to feel as if she were getting a fever again, even though her mother had given her a clean bill of health that morning. *I will not be humiliated again*, she thought.

"Look, guys," Jessica started. "Cheerleading is supposed to be fun. This program Heather just got through explaining is more like something you'd do at a military boot camp. After two days of doing this diet-and-exercise thing, you're all going to hate cheerleading. You're never going to want to pick up another pom-pom again."

"I've been wanting to get in better shape for a long time," Helen said. "I think this sounds like the perfect way to do it."

"Me too," Amy agreed.

"I'd do anything if I could have a body like Heather's," Jeannie said. "She's totally sexy, and all the guys think so."

Jessica's blood was starting to boil. "But it's only cheerleading. This isn't supposed to be something that's like life or death. Is it really worth putting yourselves through all that misery?"

"We want to go to the nationals, Jessica," Annie said. "This sounds like the best way to get there."

"Even if it means starving yourselves and putting your bodies through absolute torture?" Jessica asked in disbelief.

"Let's take a vote," Heather said. "All those in favor of following my plan and going to the nationals, raise their right hand."

Everyone raised her hand except Jessica.

"That settles it," Heather said, jumping up. "OK, hit the decks. I want seventy-five sit-ups from every one of you, and I want to see you sweat!"

Jessica watched in total amazement as every girl started doing sit-ups. The worst part was that they all looked completely happy and ecstatic to be doing them! *So much for my ultimatum*, she thought glumly.

Chapter 12

"Jessica! You look beautiful!" Mrs. Wakefield exclaimed as Jessica entered the room on Friday night.

Elizabeth's heart sank. Her sister was looking more ravishing than ever in a pale-blue sleeveless dress that fell just above her ankles. It was sophisticated yet sexy, and it showed off her lanky figure. Her hair was perfectly blown dry so that every piece fell into place, and the makeup she was wearing finished off her polished look. Even though Elizabeth knew she could look just like that if she made the effort, she still felt incredibly jealous.

"Liz, don't you have to get ready for your date with Todd?" Jessica asked as she plopped down onto a chair. "I thought you were going on one of your nerdy literary dates."

"I'm already dressed for my date," Elizabeth snapped, feeling defensive about the jeans and old sweatshirt she'd thrown on. "Todd likes me just the way I am. I don't have to put on a bunch of makeup to get him to like me."

"Well, Ken likes me just the way I am too, but that doesn't mean I want to go dressed like a janitor on our date," Jessica teased. "I mean, really, you look terrible."

"Thanks for the compliment, sister dear," Elizabeth said curtly.

"What are you and Ken doing tonight?" Mrs. Wakefield asked.

"I don't know," Jessica said dreamily. "Ken said it was a surprise. He's planned something special for our second date. I can't wait. I need a fun night after the nightmare day I had."

"Nightmare at Sweet Valley High?" Mr. Wakefield joked.

"No, really," Jessica said. "Heather Mallone is ruining my life. I talked to the girls on the squad about Maria and Sandy being fired, and they didn't care. Heather has them eating out of her hand."

"I had lunch with Maria today, and she looked pretty upset," Elizabeth said. "Maybe you should ask her to join you on your date tonight."

Jessica burst out laughing. "Yeah, right. I'm really going to ask Maria to come on my date with

Ken. I hope you're joking, because if you're not, I think you need to have the Jell-O taken out of your brain. Besides, Maria has a boyfriend. I'm sure she's seeing Winston tonight."

"Winston had to, umm . . . go visit his grandparents," Elizabeth lied. "I know she'd like the company."

"Well, if you're so worried about her, why don't you ask her to join you and *your* date?" Jessica said. "After all, she's really more your friend than she is mine."

"But I know she really feels close to you," Elizabeth tried.

"Liz, give it a rest," Jessica said, shaking her head. "She's not going on my date. Period. Finito."

Even Elizabeth had to admit to herself that that was a pretty lame way to try to ruin Jessica's date, but she was desperate. She knew there had to be some way to keep her from going out with Ken.

"Mom, don't you think Jessica still looks a little pale?" Elizabeth asked. "Maybe you're not over your sickness, Jess."

"I feel great," Jessica said. "The only thing making me sick is Heather Mallone. She's a virus of the worst kind, and I'd love to find the cure to get rid of her."

"Are you sure you feel better?" Mrs. Wakefield asked with a worried expression. "You *were* running a fever yesterday."

"I thought you were supposed to wait a couple of days after having a fever before you did too much activity," Elizabeth said. She knew her mother well enough to know that if she thought one of her kids was sick, she'd do anything to make them better. *If I get her worried enough, Mom will forbid Jessica from going on her date,* Elizabeth thought.

"I promise you, I never felt better," Jessica insisted.

"You were coughing all last night," Elizabeth lied. "I could barely sleep from all the noise coming out of your room."

"I was?" Jessica asked. "I don't remember that at all."

"I guess you were just coughing in your sleep," Elizabeth said. "You probably still have whatever bug it was that you had yesterday. I doubt Ken will really want to be exposed to it."

"Do you have the chills or anything?" Mrs. Wakefield asked, looking more and more worried. "Do you feel feverish?"

"I don't have a fever!" Jessica yelled. "Here, feel my forehead." Jessica walked over to her mom and knelt in front of her.

"You don't feel warm," Mrs. Wakefield said, putting one hand on Jessica's forehead and the other on her own.

"There. That settles it," Jessica said. "Now you can all stop worrying about me."

"I don't know," Elizabeth said, shaking her head. "You still look sick to me."

"Liz! What's with you tonight? If I didn't know better, I'd say you didn't want me to go on this date tonight!"

"Why would you ever think anything as silly as that?" Elizabeth asked innocently. "I'm just worried about you."

"Well, don't worry about me," Jessica said. "I can take care of myself. Especially with the help of the handsome Ken Matthews."

"I just heard a car pull up," Mr. Wakefield said.

Jessica looked out the window. "It's Ken!"

Elizabeth felt a wave of jealousy and sadness flood over her.

"See you guys later! Don't wait up!" Jessica called out as she jumped up and flew through the front door.

Elizabeth was sitting next to Todd at the bookstore listening to one of her favorite writers read a short story, and she had no idea what the story was about. Normally, she would have been hanging on every word, but her thoughts were miles away.

She had one thing on her mind, and it wasn't literature. *Where are they right now?* Elizabeth wondered as her eyes stared blankly at the psychology bookshelf to her right. *What does "very romantic" mean? Todd said Ken planned something "very romantic" for their date. I'm afraid that doesn't mean bowling.*

She looked at Todd, who was absorbed by the reading. Their shared interest in books and writers was one of Elizabeth's favorite things about her relationship with Todd, but now it all seemed boring. *I'm sure Ken and Jessica are doing something a lot more romantic than this right now.*

"This is great, isn't it?" Todd whispered in her ear. "Let's buy a copy of her new book when she's done."

"Yeah, great," Elizabeth whispered back.

Her guilt was unbearable. Todd was so eager to please. The reading had been her idea, and he was there jumping right into it with enthusiasm, as he did everything. *He's a great guy. Why can't I just be happy with him and forget about Ken?*

Elizabeth turned her face toward the direction of the writer and tried to plaster an interested smile on her face, but it was taking all her effort. Every now and then Todd would smile at her to acknowledge something funny or well written, and Elizabeth smiled back, even though she had no idea what she was smiling about.

After what seemed like an eternity, the audience applauded the author, and Elizabeth realized the reading was over.

"So which story did you like the most?" Todd asked.

"What do you mean?" Elizabeth asked.

"She read three different stories. I was just wondering if you liked one more than the other."

Elizabeth was so out of it that she didn't even realize that the writer had read more than one story. "Hmmmm, well, it's hard to say which one I liked best. They were all so good."

"I know what you mean," Todd said. "I think I liked the one about the old women at the post office the most."

"Yeah, that was a great one," Elizabeth said. "Do you want to browse around awhile?" She was eager to stop a detailed conversation about the stories, since it would be obvious that she hadn't been listening. She certainly didn't want to have to explain *why* she hadn't been paying attention.

"So I wonder what Ken and Jessica are up to tonight," Elizabeth said as they walked slowly through the poetry section of the bookstore. She was trying to sound as nonchalant as possible.

"Ken was really secretive about it," Todd said, pulling out a volume of Robert Frost's poems. "All he said was that he'd planned something totally romantic."

Romantic. I'm starting to hate that word, Elizabeth thought as her curiosity grew stronger by the minute. "Do you think he just meant that they were going to a movie?"

"Like I said, he was vague on the details, but from the look on his face I would imagine they're doing something pretty special," Todd said as he flipped through the pages of the book he was holding.

"Did he say anything about his feelings for Jessica?" Elizabeth asked. She pulled out a book of Adrienne Rich's poetry and flipped through the pages in an attempt to seem casual.

"Liz, you're holding that book upside down," Todd said.

Elizabeth looked at the book and saw that in fact it *was* upside down. She quickly put it back on the shelf. "I guess I'm just still thinking about those wonderful stories Kate Staples just read."

"Yeah, you seem a little spacey," Todd said, kissing her on the cheek.

"So did he say anything to you about how he feels about my sister?" Elizabeth asked again. She hated pumping him for answers like that, but since he was Ken's best friend, he was the best source for finding out the information she wanted.

"Well, it seems like he really has the hots for her," Todd said.

"How can you tell? Did he actually say that?"

"Hey, why such a big interest in Ken and Jessica?"

Because I had a fling with him when you were in Vermont, and I can't stand that he's dating my sister, Elizabeth thought miserably to herself. "Just normal sisterly concern. I guess I'm just afraid of Jessica getting hurt again. You know how awful that whole thing with Jeremy was. I just want to make sure Ken has good intentions."

"Well, you don't have anything to worry about," Todd said, taking her in his arms and hugging her tightly. "And I think it's really touching that you're so worried about your sister."

Not as touching as you think, Elizabeth thought guiltily.

"You didn't answer my question," she asked as they stood at the counter while Todd bought a signed copy of the book of short stories.

"Which question? You asked fifty already," Todd teased.

"How can you tell he has the hots for Jessica? Did he tell you that?"

169

"He didn't really come out and say it in those exact words. He didn't have to—it was written all over his face. He gets this kind of look when he mentions her name."

"What kind of look?"

"Kind of gooey and embarrassed—I guess it's a guy thing. I probably look the same way when I'm talking about you."

Elizabeth and Todd walked outside hand in hand. "So do you want to go get some ice cream at Casey's?" Todd asked.

Elizabeth didn't think she could bear having to put up a cheerful front any longer. All she wanted to do was go home and wait up for her sister. "I think I might be coming down with the same thing Jessica had. Do you mind taking me home?"

"Sure, if that's what you want. Do you want to rent a video on the way to your house? We could watch it together."

"No, I really think I just want to go to sleep. I'm sure I'll feel better tomorrow."

"OK, close your eyes," Ken said to Jessica.

Ken and Jessica had driven up the coast to a beautiful secluded beach, and they were sitting on a blanket in the moonlight.

As soon as Jessica was in Ken's car, her problems of the day started to drift slowly away. They had chatted nonstop on the drive up the coast, and Jessica didn't think she'd ever dated anyone she felt so comfortable with. It was a whole new concept to her—dating someone who is also a friend.

"You can open them now."

Jessica opened her eyes. Ken had lit two little lanterns that were on the sand, and he'd packed a gourmet meal that was spread out on the blanket. There was pasta with pesto, French bread with Brie cheese, strawberries dipped in chocolate, a Caesar salad, and chocolate cheesecake. He'd also brought along a boom box, which was playing some cool jazz.

"This is incredible! Where did you get all this?"

"I went to that new gourmet deli earlier today and asked them to pack a romantic picnic for the beach," Ken said. "I wanted tonight to be special."

"It is special," Jessica said. "And you're really special, Ken." She leaned over and kissed Ken tenderly on the lips.

Ken filled two champagne glasses with sparkling apple cider and handed one to Jessica. "I'd like to propose a toast. To the beginning of a beautiful relationship."

"You're quoting Humphrey Bogart from *Casablanca*," Jessica said with excitement. "That's my favorite movie."

"That's *my* favorite movie," Ken said, laughing. "I've seen it about five times."

"I think you're the first guy I've met who loved that movie," Jessica said. "I'm starving—let's eat."

Ken smeared a huge chunk of Brie onto a piece of French bread and handed it to Jessica. "How's that for a start?"

"Perfect," Jessica said, taking a big bite. "This definitely is *not* on Heather's starvation diet. She'd probably be horrified if she saw me eating this. I read somewhere that Brie has more fat in it than any other cheese. I'm loving every last fat gram."

"Heather's diet-and-exercise plan sounds really ridiculous," Ken said, preparing a piece of bread and Brie for himself. "If she's not careful, she's going to have a squad of anorexic cheerleaders."

"You're right," Jessica said in a serious tone. Jessica looked out at the water that was lit up by the full moon and thought about Robin and her bout with anorexia. She had gotten so thin and weak that eventually she had to be hospitalized and fed intravenously. She felt a pang of sadness. *If only Robin were still here*, she thought. *All my problems with Heather would be nonexistent. Robin would still be my cocaptain, and Sandy and Maria would still be on the squad.*

"I still can't believe that people are going along with her," Ken said. "I give them about two days of dieting and exercising before they come running back to you, demanding that you be the sole captain. I would just wait it out and let them see for themselves how terrible Heather's plan is."

"Do you really think that will happen?" Jessica asked hopefully. "Heather has them so convinced that she knows what's best for them. Maybe she does."

"Jessica, you're a great captain, and I don't want you to think for a minute that Heather knows more about cheerleading than you do. Your squad was better than ever at that Big Mesa game two weeks ago."

"Even better than last Wednesday's game?"

"A thousand times better," Ken said. "And I'm really in a position to know, since I'm on the team. What you girls do out there on the field really affects how we play. We count on that energy and support, and it was so much stronger when you were in charge than when Heather was."

"Are you just saying that to make me feel better?" Jessica asked as she studied Ken's gorgeous face in the moonlight.

"If it makes you feel better, I'm glad, but that's not why I'm saying it," Ken said. "I honestly think that."

"You're the best," Jessica said.

Ken looked deeply into Jessica's eyes and took her face in his hands. "And you're beautiful, Jessica Wakefield. If I don't kiss you right now, I'm going to have to run into the water and drown myself."

"We can't have that," Jessica teased. "Your parents would never forgive me, not to mention the football team."

Jessica closed her eyes and Ken kissed her sweetly on the lips. She felt her heart pounding, and even though she didn't really want to, she pulled herself away from Ken's embrace before they went any further.

"I think we better eat," Jessica said. "And I want you to fill up my plate with high-fat food. This girl is *not* on a diet!"

Chapter 13

Why aren't they home yet? Elizabeth wondered as she looked at her digital clock. If they went to a movie or dinner, they'd be back by now. It was after midnight, and Elizabeth was waiting up for Jessica to get home from her date. As every minute passed, her agitation and jealousy grew. She kept having images of Ken and Jessica kissing each other, and it made her feel sick to her stomach. Even though it was crazy, Elizabeth was on the verge of jumping into the Jeep and finding them.

She was also feeling incredibly guilty about Todd. He had been so sweet when he thought Elizabeth was sick after the reading. He offered to take her to the drugstore to buy her some cold medicine. It was awful lying to him the way she'd been doing, but she thought that the truth would even be worse.

Ken and Todd were best friends. There was no way Todd would ever be able to forgive Elizabeth or Ken for what had happened between them. The worst part of all was that Elizabeth was afraid she was still in love with Ken.

Elizabeth reached under her bed and pulled out her secret box. It was an old cigar box she'd covered with different kinds of wrapping paper, and inside she kept little mementos that she didn't want anyone to see. There was a corsage of dried red sweetheart roses Todd had given her the first time they'd gone to a dance together. There were five poems no one had ever seen that she'd written after she was in a car accident and Jessica's boyfriend, Sam Woodruff, had been killed. There was a little heart necklace Todd had given her in the sixth grade, and wrapped in a lace handkerchief was a picture in a frame.

She slowly untied the handkerchief and looked at the picture. When Ken and Elizabeth had been together, they'd gone to the boardwalk and had their pictures taken inside a booth. Elizabeth had put them in a purple frame, and she hadn't looked at them for months.

There were four shots. In the first they were looking at each other and laughing. *I really was happy with him,* Elizabeth thought, smiling at the memory of that day. *And I know he was happy with me too.* The next three pictures made Elizabeth ache. In all of them they were kissing.

Elizabeth lay down on her pillow and closed her eyes, clutching the frame to her chest. *He's probably kissing Jessica right now. Is he thinking of me? Is he with her because she looks like me?*

She looked at the pictures again, and she tried to go back to that day in her mind. They'd driven to an amusement park on a boardwalk about an hour from Sweet Valley. They'd wanted to find a place where nobody they knew would see them.

Elizabeth remembered how they'd spent hours sitting at an outside café on the boardwalk and talked about everything from books, to music and religion. Elizabeth had felt so light and free that day. They'd been so comfortable together.

When the sun had started going down, they'd strolled along the boardwalk, hand in hand. Except for the occasional stolen kiss at the movies, it was the only time they'd been physically affectionate in public, and it felt great. They'd stopped to play a shooting game at one of the booths, and Ken had won a big pink teddy bear, which he'd given to Elizabeth. She didn't want to have to explain to anyone where she'd gotten the bear, so she'd given it to a little girl who'd been crying by the merry-go-round.

The pictures helped Elizabeth remember that they really had been together. They were the only reminder she had. The last few times she'd seen him, Ken had been so cold and distant—as if they'd never been anything except friends. *These pictures are proof,* Elizabeth thought. *Are they all I'm ever going to have? Will Ken and I ever talk about what happened between us? Will we ever rekindle our brief but magical relationship?*

Elizabeth looked at the clock again. Twelve thirty. *I'm not going to sleep until Jessica's in this house,* Elizabeth thought, sitting up on her bed, still clutching the picture frame.

The waiting was driving her crazy, so she decided to play some music. She put on a song that Ken and she had listened to in his car on the way to the beach the day they'd had the pictures made. Ken had said that that would always be their song. It was "Unforgettable" by Natalie Cole. She listened to the song and looked at the pictures, and she imagined kissing Ken. . . .

"Elizabeth! You're still up!" Jessica flew through the door, and Elizabeth quickly hid the picture underneath her pillow.

"I didn't even hear you come in," Elizabeth

said, looking startled. "Where have you been?"

"I've been having the most wonderful time of my entire life," Jessica said dreamily. "I feel like I'm floating on air."

Jessica plopped down next to Elizabeth on her bed and took a deep breath. It was torture having to say good night to Ken in his car. She felt as if she could have stayed there all night, kissing him on the lips and feeling his hands gently stroking her neck and hair.

"Pinch me," Jessica said, holding out her arm.

"What are you talking about?" Elizabeth asked. "Why would I pinch you?"

"Because I feel like I must be dreaming," Jessica sighed. "I didn't want the night to end. We would have stayed in his car, kissing good night for hours, if we both didn't have to get up early tomorrow for the big game."

"You're home really late as it is," Elizabeth said, sounding like a mother. "You're going to be exhausted tomorrow. You shouldn't have stayed out so long."

Jessica thought that was a strange reaction, but she was too elated to give it much thought. "Ken is the most wonderful guy in the whole world," she gushed. "You're not going to believe what he did tonight."

"What?" Elizabeth asked curtly.

179

"We drove up the coast to a deserted beach and had a gourmet picnic, which Ken planned himself. He brought lanterns and music, and we danced in the moonlight. He's so romantic."

"Sounds great," Elizabeth said unenthusiastically.

"What's with you?" Jessica asked. "You seem totally unexcited for me."

"What do you want me to do? Jump up and down? Throw a party?"

What's her problem? Jessica thought. *She probably had a fight with Todd or something.* "Forget about it," Jessica said. She was too happy to let Elizabeth spoil her euphoria. "Anyway, we sat on the beach, talking about everything. He made me feel a thousand times better about that stupid Heather and the whole cheerleading situation. He's such a great listener and he gives wonderful advice. I feel like the luckiest girl on earth."

"Uh-huh," Elizabeth muttered.

"So we're sitting there under the stars, and it's like a movie," Jessica said. "He even quoted *Casablanca,* which we both said was our favorite movie."

"That's *my* favorite movie," Elizabeth snapped.

"Well, it's mine too," Jessica said. "I didn't know there was some law that says only you can have

Casablanca as your favorite movie. I mean, what's the big deal?"

"Nothing," Elizabeth said.

"Well, anyway, we're starting to eat our beautiful dinner, and Ken starts kissing me so passionately—"

"That's enough, Jessica! What makes you think I want to hear every little detail of your stupid date?" Elizabeth barked.

Jessica was stunned. *Where is this coming from? She's acting like a total crazy person.* "Liz, I thought you'd be thrilled for me. I'm sitting here telling you how happy I am, and you're being downright mean to me."

Elizabeth stood up and her body was shaking. "You're just so selfish, Jessica Wakefield. You think the whole world revolves around you, and that I have nothing else to do or think about than listen to every word that Ken said to you. For all you know, Ken might be seeing somebody else. Don't forget how deceived you were by Jeremy not so long ago. Ken could turn out to be the same way, and it will be too late because you're going so fast with him."

"But Ken is nothing like Jeremy, and I can't believe you'd say something so cruel and nasty," Jessica said. Elizabeth's words were like swords through Jessica's heart. She'd just decided to open herself up to love again, and her own sister was telling her she'd probably get hurt.

"Don't expect me to be there to pick up the pieces of your broken heart again," Elizabeth said as she stormed out of the room, slamming the door behind her.

Jessica was on the verge of tears. Only moments before she'd been happier than she'd been in months, and now her sister had made her feel absolutely miserable. She was suddenly overcome with exhaustion. She'd been trying all night to fight the sickness she knew she still had, but her sister's words made her feel physically beaten up.

She fell back on Elizabeth's pillow and felt something hard. Reaching underneath the pillow, she pulled out the picture in its frame. She turned it over, and almost choked at the images of Ken and Elizabeth kissing. *What's this? This picture must have been taken this year,* Jessica realized as she recognized a shirt Elizabeth had bought several months earlier. *No wonder she's been acting so bizarre about Ken and me.*

She was having a hard time breathing. It didn't make sense. Ken and Todd were best friends. Elizabeth didn't even seem like Ken's type. A tear rolled down Jessica's cheek. *I knew Ken was too good to be true,* she thought sadly as she remembered kissing him only moments before.

I have to find out what happened between them, Jessica decided as she put the picture back under the pillow. *But I can't do it until after the game tomorrow. I need to put this out of my mind as much as possible and concentrate on Heather Mallone. But I'm going to get to the bottom of this no matter what it takes!*

Jessica walked onto the football field before the big game against Claremont High with the determination to take back her squad. She refused to let her discovery the night before of the pictures of Ken and Jessica get her down. When she'd looked in the mirror before leaving the house, she'd said out loud, "You're Jessica Wakefield, and you're not going to let anything or anyone keep you from getting what you want. You never have in the past, and you're not going to start now."

Excited crowds filled the bleachers. It was a beautiful sunny day, and there wasn't a cloud in the sky. Jessica stood in front of the cheerleading squad with her pom-poms on her hips and gave a pep talk to the girls. Everyone was wearing the new skimpy uniforms Heather had given them, and reluctantly, Jessica was wearing hers as well. The new uniforms were creating a stir in the stands from the male fans, but Jessica tried to ignore it.

"Every one of you is a great cheerleader, and we have a fabulous football team out there, so let's show the other team what Sweet Valley High is made of," Jessica said enthusiastically. "I want you to yell louder and jump higher than you ever have before. A football team is as good as the people cheering for them!"

Jessica noticed that Heather was being unusually quiet. *Good, maybe she finally realized that I'm really the one in charge and she should just leave everything to me,* Jessica thought as she positioned herself to lead the first cheer.

She raised her pom-poms in the air and was ready to start the cheer that they always did right before the game when Heather jumped in front of her.

"Ready, girls?" Heather shouted. "One, two, three, go!"

Jessica watched in horror as they started doing a cheer that she'd never seen before. She stood to the side feeling like a total fool. The cheer was too complicated just to jump in and follow the steps. They were doing some kind of fancy dance and reciting the words as if it were a rap song. The people in the stands were snapping their fingers and clapping along, and the cheerleaders looked as if they were having a blast. At the end of the cheer the crowd was on their feet applauding and whistling wildly. *This is the last straw,* Jessica thought angrily.

"Well, Heather," she said to her cocaptain. "You finally got what you set out to do. You've been trying your best to take over my squad, and you finally did it. These girls have demonstrated that they feel no loyalty to me at all, and they've allowed you to come in and brainwash them. You'll all be happy to know that I *quit*!" Jessica threw down her pom-poms and stormed off the field.

Chapter 14

Jessica was sitting in a booth at the Dairi Burger pushing her hot-fudge sundae around on the dish with her spoon. After she'd stormed off the field that afternoon, she'd gone straight home and up to her room for a good cry. Ken had come by the house and practically dragged her out to get ice cream.

He was trying his best to cheer her up, but it wasn't working. Not only was she upset about quitting the squad, but she was still confused and devastated by the pictures she'd found the night before of him and Elizabeth. *Coming here was a big mistake,* she thought as she felt a lump in her throat. She didn't want to go out with Ken in the first place, but he'd been so forceful, and she didn't want to have to tell him about finding the pictures. She just wasn't up to it.

"I think quitting the squad was the best thing you could have done," Ken said. "I'm really proud of you."

"You are?" Jessica asked, looking up from her sundae dish. Even though Jessica was upset about the pictures, she still appreciated Ken's support. After all, she'd been talking to him more than anyone else about the whole cheerleading fiasco. *Just put the pictures out of your head for now,* she told herself.

"Absolutely. There was no way you could have continued on the squad like that," Ken said, popping a big spoonful of whipped cream into his mouth. "You would have gone completely crazy. Some people are born to be natural leaders, and you're one of those people. You don't need someone like Heather Mallone telling you what to do."

Ken's words were sweet, but they didn't make Jessica feel any better. "I still can't believe they chose Heather over me," Jessica said, eating a big bite of hot fudge and vanilla ice cream. "I mean, what does she have that I don't?"

"Nothing at all," Ken said. "She's a total loser, and I'm amazed that people can't see that. She's totally fake. I can tell that just from the way she talks to me."

"She's been pretty flirtatious with you from what I can see," Jessica said. Jessica wasn't even jealous of Ken and Heather. Her own sister was the only person she had to worry about in terms of Ken. As much as she tried to put it out of her mind, the image of them kissing each other kept creeping back. *How could he have kissed her?* she wondered as she studied Ken's face. *Did he think of Elizabeth when he was kissing me last night? Is he using me to get to Elizabeth?* She had to believe that he'd been sincere with her. More than anything else they were good friends. Ken couldn't have been pretending to be her friend . . . could he?

"And she's the worst kind of flirtatious," Ken said. "She's not at all natural like you are. And you're about ten times prettier than she is."

"Thanks," Jessica said glumly. Normally, hearing that would have made Jessica happy, but even that didn't seem to matter anymore.

"Let's go to Lila's pool party and celebrate winning the game with everyone," Ken said. "It'll be fun. I think it would cheer you up."

"You go ahead," Jessica said. "I just want to go home and be by myself." The last thing Jessica felt like doing was going to celebrate the football game. She couldn't stand the idea of facing everybody after she'd quit the squad like that. *Thank goodness tomorrow's Sunday*, Jessica thought. *I wish I never had to go back to Sweet Valley High.*

Robin's lucky—she gets to start over at a brand-new school.

"Come on, Jessica," Ken urged as they walked out of the Dairi Burger. "You have nothing to be ashamed of. I think you should hold your head high and show the world that you're stronger than ever."

"Can you just take me home?" Jessica asked, getting into Ken's car.

"Are you sure that's what you want?"

"I'm sure," Jessica said as she fought back the tears. The reality was sinking in. *I quit the cheerleading squad,* she thought in horror. *What am I if not a cheerleader?*

"Have you talked to your sister since the game?" Lila asked Elizabeth, who was standing next to Lila's pool with Todd, Enid, Winston, and Maria. "I tried calling her to make sure she was coming here tonight, but there was no answer."

"I didn't have a chance to speak to her yet," Elizabeth said. *And I'm probably the last person she wants to see right now,* she thought sadly. She hadn't talked to her sister since the night before, when Elizabeth had said those awful things about Ken. She was at the football game earlier that day and had seen Jessica quit the squad. She felt terrible for her twin. She knew how much cheerleading meant to Jessica, and she knew her sister must be feeling awful.

"I'm so glad she did that," Maria said. "Heather is a horrible person, and she just totally stole the control of the squad out from under Jessica. She's better off not having anything to do with those girls, since they didn't show her any kind of loyalty."

"I agree," Lila said. "Look at the way Heather's flirting with the entire football team in the pool. I didn't even invite her to my party, but there she is."

"She was making me sick the way she acted like a movie star after the game," Maria said. "She kept bouncing from one interviewer to another, taking all the credit for the team's success."

"I noticed that too," Winston said. "She acted like she was the quarterback of the football team."

"Speaking of the quarterback—I'm surprised Ken isn't here," Lila said. "I guess he's trying to cheer up Jessica. I'm glad she has him right now."

For the first time since Jessica and Ken had started dating, Elizabeth didn't feel jealous. She, too, was glad that Jessica had Ken to talk to. She felt guilty not only because of Ken, but also because she hadn't really been there for Jessica when she had wanted to talk about Heather and the cheerleading problems she was having. *I'm the one who told her to make Heather a cocaptain in the first place*, she thought.

"I can't even imagine your sister not being a cheerleader," Todd said.

"I know what you mean," Winston agreed. "When I think of Jessica, I automatically think of cheerleading."

Elizabeth felt so far away from Jessica. The fact that she'd kept a secret from her created an enormous gulf between them. Usually when Jessica had a problem, Elizabeth was right there to bail her out. Because of the distance Elizabeth had created, she hadn't been there for her sister when Jessica had needed her the most. *Maybe I should just tell her about what happened between Ken and me,* Elizabeth thought. *Keeping a secret like this from her feels wrong, and if it goes on any longer, it could ruin our relationship for good!*

As soon as Ken dropped Jessica off at her house, she went right up to Elizabeth's room. She knew that Elizabeth would be at Lila's party and that her parents had gone to dinner with friends. She didn't know what she was looking for, but she was determined to find out more about her sister and Ken.

Jessica knew that Elizabeth always kept a diary of everything that happened to her. In the past Jessica would have thought her sister's life was too boring to read about, but now she was desperate to find her diary. *Apparently, there are things I never knew about Elizabeth,* Jessica thought as she felt a chill through her whole body.

Where does she keep that stupid diary? Jessica wondered as she searched Elizabeth's desk. She looked in the closet and on Elizabeth's bookshelf, but she found nothing. She got down on the floor and looked under Elizabeth's bed. *There it is,* she thought as she grabbed the red leather book and sat down on the bed.

Her hands were shaking as she opened the diary to the first page. She wasn't sure she really wanted to find out the truth about Ken. He'd made her so happy, and she hated to let go of that.

She also knew that if she didn't find out what happened, the doubts and suspicion would always haunt her.

Jessica skimmed through the first few pages of the diary, and it appeared to be mostly about the books Elizabeth was reading or the tests she was studying for. *How typical of Elizabeth to write down every boring little detail of her boring life,* Jessica thought as she continued to flip the pages.

Then her eyes settled on three letters: K-E-N! And to Jessica's horror his name was all over the diary! Her hands were shaking, and she felt the sweat start to form on her brow.

Ken called me this afternoon, and we went to a movie tonight. It almost seemed like a Saturday-night date, but of course he's just looking after me like Todd asked him to. Still, when he dropped me off at my house afterward, I wasn't expecting to feel the way I did as I looked into his eyes to say good-bye....

Jessica's eyes skipped ahead frantically to more passages about Ken. As painful as it was to read about her sister's feelings for Ken, she couldn't resist.

The backyard was dark, and we slipped eagerly into the shadows. Without another word Ken folded his arms around me, lifting me slightly so his mouth could find mine. I kissed him hungrily, my fingers tangling in his hair. Meanwhile, his hands were on my neck, my shoulders, my back. We couldn't seem to stop touching each other— maybe because for weeks we'd been dying to do this, but holding back.

Jessica dropped the diary onto the floor and collapsed onto Elizabeth's bed in tears. It was true—Elizabeth had had an affair with Ken while Todd had been in Vermont. Jessica's feelings were so jumbled up and confused that she didn't know which emotion was stronger—her jealousy, or the feeling of being betrayed by a sister who had kept a secret from her.

This has truly been the worst day of my life, Jessica thought. *I'm not a cheerleader anymore, and the person I thought was becoming my new boyfriend had an affair with my sister!*

Don't miss SVH #113: **The Pom-pom Wars**, *the next book in this sensational three-part mini-series!*

It's Your
First Love. . .
Yours *and* His.

Love Stories

Nobody Forgets
Their First Love!

Now there's a romance series that gets to the heart of *every-one's* feelings about falling in love. Love Stories reveals how boys feel about being in love, too! In every story, a boy and girl experience the real-life ups and downs of being a couple, and share in the thrills, joys, and sorrows of first love.

MY FIRST LOVE, Love Stories #1
0-553-56661-X $3.50/$4.50 Can.

SHARING SAM, Love Stories #2
0-553-56660-1 $3.50/$4.50 Can.

Coming in February 1995

Bantam Doubleday Dell
Books for Young Readers   BFYR 104-7/94

Here's an excerpt from
Love Stories #2,

Sharing Sam

SOME PEOPLE SAID Sam had robbed a Get 'n' Go in Okeechobee. Some said he was an undercover narc. A reliable source in the girls' bathroom claimed he was Mick Jagger's illegitimate son. We were bored with our gentle lives, and dark, silent Sam was the object of much speculation. As the new guy at school and the only male in AP Bio to sport a black leather jacket, he was asking for it.

Sam rode a motorcycle, no helmet. In the sea of entry-level Chevy sedans and sober parent-mobiles, the big Harley in Student Lot B commanded attention. It spoke of mangled limbs, decapitations, promising lives cut short. Conjugating verbs from my window seat in Spanish class, I couldn't take my eyes off it.

I suppose, given that Harley, not to mention the rumors, that it didn't surprise me when I happened, one Monday after school, to witness Sam Cody's inevitable demise.

I was sitting under a tree in the middle of an orange grove near my house. Snickers, my Arabian mare, was grazing nearby. The day, warm and clear, dazzled like a prism. I had my history textbook open on my lap, which I figured was almost the same thing as reading it.

I went to the grove from time to time—sometimes to study, more often to daydream. The star of my reveries was Lance Potts, the golden-boy-blue-eyed-honor-society-junior-class-president-football-center guy I'd fantasized about for months, practicing pillow kisses after *SNL* on Saturday nights. Although Lance had no idea I existed, he was always kind enough to make an appearance in my daydreams at a moment's notice.

But lately Sam Cody had been making unscheduled appearances in them as well. I was not sure what to make of this development. Sam was not, after all, the kind of guy I was attracted to.

Although, to be fair, Sam did have very nice eyes.

The hoarse whine of a motorcycle broke the stillness. I tossed my book aside. This was not a bike trail. Technically, it wasn't even a horse trail. Yelling a few expletives, I dashed out to the narrow dirt road that bisected the grove. Then I saw the black jacket, the too-long hair, and I knew it was Sam.

It was one thing to ponder Sam's dark history over a bowl of Orville Redenbacher's Light on a dateless Friday evening. It was quite another thing to be trapped in the middle of nowhere with him, armed only with my pepper spray, the one my mom had stuck in the toe of my stocking the Christmas before.

"Hey!" I screamed. "Get off the trail!"

Suddenly, as if he'd reined it in at my command, the bike bucked and twisted. It careened off the trail, carving a clean arc in the still air. Sam clung to it like a bronco rider as the bike plummeted to the ground near an orange tree. It somersaulted once before coming to a stop.

The Harley silenced, the field came alive again with chirps, buzzes, whirs. I waited, hoping for a moan, some sign he'd survived.

Nothing.

As I ran to the wreck, I steeled myself for the bloodied corpse and lifeless stare, the horror-movie scenes from those driver's ed movies. I conjured up pages from my first-aid book. A, B,

C: A was airway, B was breathing, but what the heck was C?

The grass stirred.

Sam was wrapped around the twisted carcass of his bike. A tiny trickle of blood made its way down his left temple.

He opened his eyes. "This isn't hell, is it?"

I shook my head, incredibly relieved that he was alive.

"Florida," I said.

"Close enough."

"I'm here to rescue you," I said nervously. "Don't move."

I leaned close to check his eyes. If his pupils were dilated, that was a bad thing, although I couldn't remember why. Close up, his face was all angles and planes, a geometry lesson. His eyes were nearly black, thick brows, thick lashes. I couldn't be sure about the pupil situation. I caught the faint, acrid smell of tobacco. It figured he would smoke.

I examined a gash on his left hand. "You have a death wish or something?" I muttered.

He touched his bloody temple and swore. "I blew a damn tire. I can't believe it. I just changed that tire two weeks ago! Oh, man, this sucks."

"I mean, why don't you wear a helmet, for

God's sake? It's the law. Plus," I added, "you smoke."

Sam stared at me as if I weren't quite in focus. "I'm lying here bleeding to death, and you're *nagging* me?"

"I hope you realize how lucky it is you landed in a hunk of grass. It could have been a hunk of rock."

"Lucky. Yeah."

"Don't move, I have to think. I took first aid in Girl Scouts, but that was seven years ago."

Sam started to pull his leg free. He winced.

"Stop!" I cried. "Don't move the victim."

"*I'm* not the victim," he said, stroking a twisted fender.

I checked his head wound. It was bleeding, all right, although not very dramatically. I needed something to bind the cut. There was only one thing to do. I took off my T-shirt. Fortunately, I had a bathing suit top on underneath.

"Maybe I'm in heaven after all," Sam said.

I tried to rip the T-shirt with my teeth. It always works in the movies.

The movies, it just so happens, are full of crap.

"I'm Sam Cody, by the way."

"I know," I said, and was instantly sorry. Strictly speaking, there was no reason I should know his name.

"And you're Alison Chapman."

I blinked, my mouth full of T-shirt. Strictly speaking, there was no reason he should know my name.

I could feel my throat starting to blotch. It was tacky to flirt while binding a wound.

"I'm just going to tie this sucker around your head," I said. Before he could fuss, I crouched behind him, folded the shirt into a long strip, and tied it around his forehead. The back of his hair curled sweetly over his collar.

"Ow." He winced. "Just my luck I get the Brownie paramedic."

I stood, brushed off my knees, and admired my handiwork. "You may go into shock at any moment," I said. "I think I'm supposed to cover you with a blanket."

"You could use your jeans," he suggested helpfully.

"I'm going to go get my horse. I'll put her blanket over you, then ride for help. But you have to promise not to move—"

"Time out." Before I could stop him, Sam pulled free of his bike and struggled to his feet. "This is getting way too weird."

204

"I told you not to stand. You've had a brush with death."

"You did say horse?"

"Snickers. She's over there, under a tree. This is a horse trail, no bikes allowed."

"I was just passing through," he said. "It's a great shortcut to the highway."

"Didn't you see the sign?"

"Yeah, it said No Trespassing. What's your excuse?"

"I trespassed on a horse, at least."

"Can your horse do one twenty?"

"No." I kicked his blown-out tire. "But neither can your bike anymore."

Suddenly he looked infinitely sad, and I felt like a jerk.

"Look, if you're not going to sit here and wait for an ambulance, let me at least give you a ride," I said.

"I don't do horses. Look, thank you for saving my life. If you need someone to testify for your merit badge, give me a call. But I'm cool." He yanked off the T-shirt. It was smeared with blood. "Sorry," he said. "I'll buy you another one. I'm a little short on cash right now, though."

He stared at the bike forlornly. I wondered if I'd ever looked at anything with that much longing.

205

"I'm sure it can be fixed," I said.

"Maybe."

"You know someone who can tow it?"

"I'll figure something out." He took off his black jacket and slung it over his shoulder. I noticed a little plastic packet of Kleenex in one of the pockets. It seemed so incongruous that I grinned. Somehow I'd expected something more sinister.

"What?"

"Nothing. I mean, just . . . your Kleenex."

He blinked. "My what?"

"Nothing."

"Well . . . nice bleeding on you."

He limped off down the trail. His scuffed boots made little dust clouds. Sam Cody, of the wild speculation and hushed rumors, who had maybe killed a man or robbed a bank or sold substances door to door, and I don't mean vacuums.

Still, he looked sort of pathetic, his metal steed dead by the wayside.

By the time I caught up with him, he was nearly to the tree where Snickers was tied. "Come on," I said. "You might as well hitch. We're going the same way."

Sam stopped. His hair was matted where the blood had dried. He looked very tired. "Look, I don't even know you."

206

"You know my name."

"Sixth-period study hall. Two rows up, one seat over. I'm familiar with the back of your head. Yesterday you wore one of those wormy ponytail things."

"A scrunchie," I confirmed.

He narrowed his eyes. "So how is it that you know my name?"

"I've heard . . . talk."

"What kind of talk?"

"You know. You're the new guy, it's a small school, people talk."

"Yeah. Well." It was obvious he didn't give a damn.

I hesitated. Up close, with the blood, the dirt, the sweat trickling down his temples, he did look more menacing. Older than all the other guys at school, with their dust-bunny mustaches and self-conscious swaggers.

"Have you ever been to Okeechobee?" I asked.

Sam closed his eyes. I had the feeling I was wearing him out. He swayed slightly, and the Girl Scout in me took over.

I grabbed his arm, and he more or less followed along. His skin was damp and hot, but then, it was hot for January. Besides, my hands were sweating, so it's hard to know who was responsible.

207

Snickers looked him over doubtfully. Sam leaned against the trunk of the tree. His face was gray.

"This is Snickers," I said. "She's old and she's been known to bite. She doesn't like men."

"That's okay. I don't like horses," he said, but he stroked her shoulder anyway. She snorted derisively.

"Here's the deal," I said. I turned the left stirrup for him. "Left foot in here, right leg over, I'll drive. Got it?"

"I have ridden before. My grandfather has a horse. I just like my transportation without teeth."

Sam eased up into the saddle. I stuffed my book in my backpack, handed it to Sam, and climbed up behind him.

"Are you sure you're not going into shock or something?" I asked, taking the reins. "You look sort of . . . well, like you're dying, to be blunt."

"Nothing an aspirin won't cure."

I took it at a walk, afraid to jostle him any more than necessary. Holding the reins necessitated the occasional wrist-to-waist contact. My wrist, his hard, warm waist. I could smell sweat and tobacco and grass and skin, all mixed in with horse. Sounds awful, I know. It wasn't.

We fell into a smooth, gentle back-and-forth roll that was all Snickers's doing. My breasts grazed Sam's back, my thighs his thighs. Sounds harmless, I know. It wasn't.

Something was happening, something I didn't want to think about too hard. I couldn't say why, but I had the feeling Lance Potts was being retired from active daydream duty.

Lance had the résumé, he had the dimpled smile and the blue eyes. But it was Sam who was giving me goose bumps in eighty-degree Florida sunshine.

We rode so silently that I half wondered if Sam had lapsed into a coma. When we got to the highway, I reined Snickers to a halt. "I live a mile down," I said. "I could give you a lift to the doctor."

"No doctor," Sam said.

"Why not?"

"No money."

"I could lend—"

Sam hefted himself off the saddle, swinging a leg over Snickers's neck. He landed with a grimace.

"Where do you live, anyway? I wouldn't mind—"

"I'll hitch, thanks."

"You can't hitch."

209

He looked up, squinting against the after-noon glare. "Oh? Why's that?"

"You'll end up by the side of the road in a mangled heap. Not unlike your motorcycle."

"I'm a big boy. I'll take my chances."

"You take too many chances," I said, doing an uncanny impersonation of my mother. I dismounted and grabbed my pack from Sam. "Here," I said. "Let me at least give you cab money."

"No."

"A quarter for the phone?"

For the first time, Sam smiled. He touched my shoulder. "I'll be okay, Alison."

I momentarily forgot how to respond, so I kept busy digging through my backpack for some cash. While I did, Sam sauntered over to Snickers. He whispered something in her ear, something she must have liked, because normally she won't let a guy within three feet of her head. He leaned close and kissed her gently on the muzzle, and I felt myself coming to some kind of very important decision.

He caught me looking, and I pulled out a ten-dollar bill. "Here," I said. "At least take this."

But by then Sam was already heading down the road, thumb outstretched, sizing up the possibilities whizzing past.

I watched as he grew smaller and smaller, until at last a battered red pickup stopped and Sam hopped into the cab. It roared off, kicking up dust.

I wondered if he would survive the drive, the day, the year. I hoped so, because I had the insane feeling I was in distinct danger of falling in love.

Bantam Books in the Sweet Valley High series
Ask your bookseller for the books you have missed

SIGN UP FOR THE
SWEET VALLEY HIGH®
FAN CLUB!

Hey, girls! Get all the gossip on Sweet
Valley High's® most popular teenagers
when you join our fantastic Fan Club!
As a member, you'll get all of this really
cool stuff:

- Membership Card with your own
  personal Fan Club ID number
- A Sweet Valley High® Secret
  Treasure Box
- Sweet Valley High® Stationery
- Official Fan Club Pencil (for secret
  note writing!)
- Three Bookmarks
- A "Members Only" Door Hanger
- Two Skeins of J. & P. Coats® Embroidery
  Floss with flower barrette instruction
  leaflet

- Two editions of *The Oracle* newsletter
- Plus exclusive Sweet Valley High®
  product offers, special savings,
  contests, and much more!

- -

Be the first to find out what Jessica & Elizabeth Wakefield are up to by joining the
Sweet Valley High® Fan Club for the one-year membership fee of only $6.25 each
for U.S. residents, $8.25 for Canadian residents (U.S. currency). Includes shipping
& handling.

Send a check or money order (do not send cash) made payable to "Sweet Valley
High® Fan Club" along with this form to:

SWEET VALLEY HIGH® FAN CLUB, BOX 3919-B, SCHAUMBURG, IL 60168-3919

NAME_____
(Please print clearly)

ADDRESS_____

CITY_____ STATE_____ ZIP_____
(Required)

AGE_____ BIRTHDAY_____/_____/_____

Offer good while supplies last. Allow 6-8 weeks after check clearance for delivery. Addresses without ZIP
codes cannot be honored. Offer good in USA & Canada only. Void where prohibited by law.
©1993 by Francine Pascal   LCI-1383-193

Life after high school gets even *Sweeter!*

Jessica and Elizabeth are now freshmen at Sweet Valley University, where the motto is: Welcome to college — welcome to freedom!

Don't miss any of the books in this fabulous new series.

♥ College Girls #1	0-553-56308-4	$3.50/$4.50 Can.
♥ Love, Lies and Jessica Wakefield #2	0-553-56306-8	$3.50/$4.50 Can.
♥ What Your Parents Don't Know #3	0-553-56307-6	$3.50/$4.50 Can.
♥ Anything for Love #4	0-553-56311-4	$3.50/$4.50 Can.
♥ A Married Woman #5	0-553-56309-2	$3.50/$4.50 Can.
♥ The Love of Her Life #6	0-553-56310-6	$3.50/$4.50 Can.

Bantam Doubleday Dell
Books for Young Readers

Bantam Doubleday Dell
Dept. SVU 12
2451 South Wolf Road
Des Plaines, IL 60018

Please send the items I have checked above. I am enclosing $_____ (please add $2.50 to cover postage and handling). Send check or money order, no cash or C.O.D.s please.

Name _____

Address _____

City _____ State _____ Zip _____

Please allow four to six weeks for delivery.
Prices and availability subject to change without notice.   SVU 12 4/94